Nightmare in Nantucket

Garden Girls
Cozy Mystery Series Book 14

Hope Callaghan

hopecallaghan.com

This book is a work of fiction. Although places mentioned may be real, the characters, names and incidents, and all other details are products of the author's imagination and are fictitious. Any resemblance to actual events or actual persons, living or dead is purely coincidental.

Thank you, Peggy H., Cindi G., Jean P., Wanda D. and Barbara W., for taking the time to preview *Nightmare in Nantucket,* for the extra sets of eyes and for catching all my mistakes.

A special thanks to my reader review team: Alice, Amary, Barbara, Becky, Becky B, Brinda, Cassie, Christina, Debbie, Denota, Devan, Francine, Grace, Jan, Jo-Ann, Joeline, Joyce, Jean K., Jean M., Kathy, Lynne, Megan, Melda, Kat, Linda, Lynne, Pat, Patsy, Renate, Rita, Rita P, Shelba, Tamara and Vicki

Visit my website for new releases and special offers: hopecallaghan.com

TABLE OF CONTENTS

Therefore, as God's chosen people, holy and dearly loved, clothe yourselves with compassion, kindness, humility, gentleness and patience.

Bear with each other and forgive one another if any of you has a grievance against someone. Forgive as the Lord forgave you. *Colossians 3:12-13 (NIV)*

Chapter 1

Gloria Rutherford-Kennedy stared out the window of Dot's Restaurant as she gazed at the parking lot in front. "What is taking Ruth so long?"

She glanced at her watch and then began drumming her fingers on the table.

Gloria's best friend, Lucy Carlson, placed her hand over the top of Gloria's hand. "Stop doing that. It's driving me crazy."

Dot Jenkins, the co-owner of Dot's Restaurant, refilled Gloria's coffee cup before setting the carafe on the table and settling into an empty chair next to her friend. "Why don't you just tell us what the big news is?"

Gloria had called a "Garden Girls" meeting at Dot's Restaurant, claiming they needed to meet ASAP and that there was some sort of crisis. All of the women, Lucy, Dot, Margaret, Gloria, and the still "MIA" Ruth were scheduled to meet at Dot's at one o'clock on the dot.

But Ruth, the head postmaster at Belhaven, Michigan's post office, still hadn't arrived and she was late. Fifteen minutes and counting.

"If Ruth doesn't hurry up, I'm going to drive to her house and drag her here," Gloria vowed.

"It is a Saturday," Margaret pointed out. "Maybe she had some errands to run." The words were no more out of Margaret's mouth and Gloria spotted Ruth's van ease into an empty parking spot, right in front of the large picture window.

"There she is." Gloria watched as the driver's side door flew open. Ruth hopped out of the van and hurried through the door of the restaurant.

"Sorry I'm late," she said breathlessly. "I was having a vehicle-related crisis." Ruth yanked out a chair across from Gloria, dropped her purse on the floor and plopped down. "What's the 911?"

Rose Morris, the new co-owner of Dot's Restaurant, hurried over. "Did I miss anything?"

"Not yet," Lucy, Dot and Margaret said in unison.

Rose pulled a chair from the empty table next to theirs and Lucy and Margaret scooched to the side to let her in. "Spill the beans!"

All eyes turned to Gloria, anxiously waiting to find out what their friend had deemed so important that she called an emergency meeting. "It's about Andrea. Brian called me first thing this morning. Andrea is refusing to return to Belhaven. She told him she thinks she wants to call off the engagement."

An echo of horrified gasps escaped the Garden Girls' lips.

"You're kidding," Ruth said.

"Nope." Gloria shook her head. "She told Brian she was confused."

"Cold feet." Dot decided.

"Is she still upset he couldn't remember her after the accident?" Lucy asked.

Andrea Malone, the women's close friend, was engaged to Brian Sellers, deemed one of *the* most eligible bachelors in their small town. It was a match made in heaven; at least Gloria was convinced God had a hand in bringing the two together.

Brian, a former circuit court judge, had moved to the small town after inheriting his grandparents' home on nearby Lake Terrace. He had purchased several downtown businesses including the Quik Stop, Belhaven's corner grocery, along with the town's only drug store, as well as Nails and Knobs, the hardware store.

Not long ago, Brian had been attacked inside his hardware store. The attacker had knocked Brian unconscious and injured him so badly, he'd been hospitalized and suffered from amnesia.

He'd been released from the hospital and was healing nicely; but a small piece of his memory, the one that included his fiancée, Andrea, was the last to return. After doctors assured Brian he was on the mend, at least physically, a wounded and heartbroken Andrea decided to join her parents, who were vacationing on the island of Nantucket.

Not long after Andrea left, Brian's full memory returned and he couldn't wait to call Andrea to share the wonderful news. Everyone believed Andrea would return home and the couple would move forward with their plans for an upcoming engagement party followed by the wedding, set for late summer.

At least Gloria believed that until Brian had called her that morning in a state of panic.

"Brian needs to get his butt to Nantucket and haul the stubborn woman back here," Rose said.

"He can't," Gloria said. "Because of his recent concussion, the doctors don't want him flying or traveling, at least not alone."

She went on. "We can't let this happen. Those two should be together. I think Andrea's pride took a hit."

"Let me guess," Margaret said. "Her parents are encouraging the break-up."

Gloria sighed. "Reading between the lines that would be my guess."

Andrea's parents had visited several months ago. They didn't like Belhaven, they didn't like the small town, they didn't like their only child living in another state and Gloria had a sneaky suspicion they didn't like her friends, either.

The women tossed around different ideas including a phone intervention, a chat with Andrea's parents, which they quickly agreed would be a complete waste of time, and in fact, might make matters worse.

"What if we take a road trip, drive to Massachusetts and talk some sense into Andrea?" Dot asked.

"She's on an island," Gloria said.

"Surely they have commuter planes or ferry boats," Margaret said.

"I think we should do it," Ruth declared. "I'll be a designated driver but if we all plan to go, we'll need a second vehicle."

Gloria frowned. "Annabelle's new engine could use a road trip. Break it in, so to speak. Paul will want to go, too," she added.

Margaret slapped the palm of her hand on the table. "A road trip!" She smiled at Gloria. "Remember our last road trip?"

Gloria rolled her eyes. "How could I forget?"

"Yeah," Lucy piped up. "Now it's our turn to go."

The women excitedly discussed the possibility of hitting the road to rescue their friend from her parents' evil clutches.

Rose was the one to burst the bubble of excitement. "What if Brian doesn't want us to butt in?"

"You mean mind our own business?" Dot asked. "You're probably right."

"I'll check with him right now." Gloria grabbed her purse off the table and slid her chair back. "Let me make a quick phone call." She darted out of the restaurant and made her way onto the sidewalk.

Gloria pulled her cell phone from her purse. First, she had to check with Paul. It was possible he would be against them "helping" out. She dialed the house phone and waited. Thankfully, a breathless Paul answered.

"Hello dear."

"I hope you don't answer the phone like that every time," Gloria joked.

"Only when it's my lovely wife calling." Paul had convinced Gloria they needed caller id. At first, she'd balked, but after he had installed it, she loved it.

"Good answer," she replied. "What do you think about taking a road trip to Massachusetts to bring Andrea home?" she blurted out.

Paul and Gloria had been in the kitchen eating breakfast when Brian had phoned with the disturbing news and Paul had even encouraged

Gloria to meet with her friends to discuss the dilemma.

There was a long pause on the other end of the line and Gloria knew her husband was thinking. While Gloria could be impulsive, Paul was the methodical one. He liked to mull things over before making a decision, especially when it involved a plan his wife and her friends hatched.

Gloria hurriedly continued. "Not just us but all of us. All the girls plus Brian and you."

"What does Brian think?" Paul asked.

"I haven't talked to him yet," Gloria said. "I figured I should run it by you first." She knew it would please Paul since she rarely thought to run things by her husband. She was more of a "fly by the seat of her pants" person.

"I have a feeling if Brian says he thinks it's a good idea, I won't be able to talk you out of making the trip," Paul said. "So I guess I say if Brian is okay with it, I'll go along."

"Oh! I love you so much," Gloria said. "You're the best husband a woman could ever want. I'm calling Brian now. See you soon." She disconnected the line and with trembling fingers, dialed Brian's cell phone.

Unfortunately, the call went to voice mail and Gloria didn't want to share her idea in a message so she asked him to return the call as soon as possible.

Gloria began to pace the sidewalk, waiting for Brian to return the call. She passed by Ruth's van and then stopped abruptly in front of it. There was something different about Ruth's van, something she couldn't quite put her finger on.

She shifted her head and gazed at the side before taking a step closer when her cell phone began to ring. It was Brian.

"Thanks for calling me back," she said. "The girls and I have come up with a brilliant idea."

Chapter 2

"What kind of idea?" Brian asked, his voice full of suspicion and for good reason.

"An old-fashioned, cross country road trip to rescue your betrothed from the clutches of her well-intentioned, yet misguided parents," Gloria said.

"She's on an island." Brian said the first thing that popped into his head. "And I can't fly."

"You can take a ferry, though," Gloria argued.

For the second time in a row, the man on the other end of the line was quiet. Brian, like Paul, liked to think things through before making a commitment.

"I dunno," Brian finally said. "What about Paul? You're going to leave him home?"

"Nope. He's going with us."

"Huh." Gloria could tell by the tone of Brian's voice that he still wasn't convinced.

"Look," she said. "Andrea is hurt. She needs her knight in shining armor to gallop in on his white horse and whisk her away."

"And live happily ever after," Brian said. "Let me think about it."

"Fair enough," Gloria said. "Call me back as soon as possible. We've got plans to make." She disconnected the line before he had a chance to reply.

She stepped back inside the restaurant and several sets of eyes followed her across the room.

"Well?" Ruth asked. "What did he say?"

Gloria eased into her seat. She pulled her cell phone from her purse and placed it on the table before dropping her purse next to her chair. "Paul said yes and Brian said maybe."

"We're in," Rose announced. "Dot and I already ran it by Johnnie and Ray. They said they'll stay here and hold down the fort." She leaned forward and lowered her voice. "I think they're looking forward to having us out of their hair."

Lucy snorted and Dot shot her friend a death look.

"We'll have to find a place to stay," Gloria said. "I told Brian to let me know his decision as soon as possible."

The women discussed the logistics of the road trip and made the unanimous decision Gloria and Ruth would be the designated drivers.

Gloria pointed out the front window. "Ruth, your van looks different."

"Wait'll you see what I did," Ruth said.

Before she could elaborate, Gloria's cell phone chirped.

"It's Brian," Gloria grabbed her phone, pressed answer and then the speaker button. "Hi Brian. I've got you on speaker."

"Hello ladies." Brian's deep voice echoed from the phone.

"Well?" Dot asked. "What's the verdict?"

"I tried to call Andrea, to tell her we were coming...all of us, but she didn't answer. In fact, I sent her a text late yesterday and she never replied." There was a long pause on the other end of the line. "She must really want to end our relationship. Now she's not taking my calls."

Andrea had been upset but so far, she hadn't outright avoided Brian. It seemed out of character and Gloria vowed to call her after she got home.

Brian continued. "I figured if I said no, you would go without me, so the answer is yes," he said. "When do we leave?"

Rose pumped her fist in the air. "Yippee! A Garden Girls road trip."

Gloria gazed around the table. “We don’t want to take too long, but we need to get ready. Let’s leave bright and early Monday morning.”

Gloria told Brian she would call him later. She disconnected the call and turned to Margaret. “Shouldn’t you run the trip by Don first?” Don was Margaret’s husband.

“Nah.” Margaret waved her hand. “He’ll probably be thrilled to have me gone for a few days and will decide to camp out over at the country club’s clubhouse.” Margaret’s husband was a golf fanatic, which was putting it mildly.

During the summer months, Don spent most of his waking hours at Montbay Hills Golf Club. Margaret and he were members of the exclusive, members-only club. “I’ll be the unofficial trip planner and start researching the local hotels,” Margaret offered. “There must be a ferry that shuttles visitors to the island so I’ll research that, as well.”

"I say we meet here early Monday, around 6:00 a.m. and hit the road," Dot suggested.

Lucy studied the front of her cell phone. "I mapped the distance. It's almost 900 miles and 14 ½ hours from Belhaven to Massachusetts."

"We'll need to be on the road at six on the dot if we want to make it to Massachusetts in one day."

With a plan in place and an agreed-upon departure time, the group gathered their belongings and stood.

There was a lot to do in a short amount of time and Gloria's head was spinning. She bent down, picked up her purse and began to push her chair in when she suddenly realized they were forgetting someone, someone who was very important to Andrea...her former housekeeper and housemate, Alice.

"What about Alice?" Gloria asked and then shot Rose a quick glance. Rose and Alice had started out on the wrong foot. They weren't "enemies" per se, but neither were they friends.

"Tolerated" one another would be a better word used to describe the women's relationship. Still, they couldn't leave Alice behind. They would have to invite her. They needed to invite her. Alice was like a second mother to Andrea.

"I'll stop by the house to talk to her." Gloria wasn't sure if Alice was working. For several months, Alice had worked at "At Your Service," a dog-training center located not far from Belhaven.

Ruth led the way and the women followed her out of the restaurant and onto the sidewalk. Gloria trailed behind and waited for the door to close before joining the others.

She caught a glimpse of Ruth's van, which reminded her there was something different about her friend's vehicle. Gloria eased past Dot and stood in front of the chrome bumper. "What did you do to your van?"

Dot craned her neck and studied her friend's van. "It looks different."

"It's shiny," Lucy said. "Did you wax it?"

"It's shiny and there's something sticking out of the top." Margaret pointed to the roof of the van.

"Check this out!" Ruth hurried to the driver's side of the van, opened the door and slid behind the wheel. Seconds later, a round bubble popped out of the top.

Surrounding the bubble were small lenses. The lenses reminded Gloria of eyeballs. "What in the world?"

Ruth leaned out of the open door. "Smile. You're on camera."

The women circled the front of the van and stared at the contraption. Seconds later, the device disappeared and the only thing visible was a small round bump.

Ruth scrambled out of the van and slammed the door before making her way back onto the sidewalk. "It's a recording device. I just had it installed, which was why I was late."

Gloria wrinkled her nose. "Recording? What on earth are you recording?"

"It's for street maps. I signed up for a part-time job working weekends where I drive up and down back roads and streets, recording everything."

"You already have a job," Dot pointed out. "Working at the post office."

"Yeah, but my job can be boring." Ruth clasped her hands together and gazed at her vehicle admiringly. "This is so much more exciting."

"Oh, I get it." Rose shoved a fisted hand on her hip. "You're working for one of those companies who hire people to drive around, recording the streets and then it ends up on the internet."

"The drive by," Lucy said. "What a perfect job for you, Ruth."

Ruth had a knack...well, an obsession, with spy and surveillance equipment. Gloria could see where this would be right up her friend's alley. "After all these years, you've finally found your calling," she teased.

"That's not all." Ruth ran her hand over the hood of her van. "I'm also testing a new bulletproof coating for this company I found online. It's called a D65 shield."

Lucy patted the hood. "I'd love to bring my Ruger Super Redhawk over and take a shot at it."

"You want to shoot at my van?" Ruth clutched her chest. "That's crazy."

Lucy frowned. "I thought it was bulletproof."

"That's why you volunteered to be one of the designated drivers for this road trip," Gloria guessed. "So you could test all the new gadgets."

"Yep." Ruth eyed Lucy nervously. "Not only that, the company has given me a gas per diem so we won't have to cover the cost out of pocket."

"Lordy." Rose placed a hand on both sides of her cheeks and shook her head as she gazed at Ruth's bulletproof, camera recording, souped-up set of wheels. "What have I gotten myself into?"

"Don't worry." Dot patted Rose's shoulder. "We'll take good care of you."

"This will be one road trip you won't soon forget," Margaret predicted. "Not if it involves Gloria."

"Paul will keep us in line," Gloria said as she glanced at her watch. "I better head over to Andrea's place to see if I can track down Alice." She climbed into her car and with a small wave to her friends who were still standing on the sidewalk in front of Dot's Restaurant, she backed out of the parking spot and pulled onto Main Street.

Gloria drove up the hill and then turned right onto Andrea's gravel drive. She eased Annabelle past the metal gate.

Alice, who had passed her driving exam and gotten her driver's license a few months back, had recently purchased an older four-door sedan.

The gray car was sitting in the drive and Gloria parked Annabelle behind the car. She dropped her car keys into her purse and strode to the mini-mansion's front double doors. It took a few raps on the brass knocker, as well as several doorbell rings before a harried Alice swung the front door open.

"Miss Gloria. I'm so glad you stopped by," Alice said. "I was just going to give you a call." She grasped Gloria's hand and pulled her into the house. "I try to call Andrea yesterday and today, but she no answer," she said in her thick Spanish accent. "I try her parents, but they no answer their phone either."

Brian's words echoed in Gloria's head, how Andrea had not answered when he had tried calling her. She hadn't replied to his text either.

"Let me try." Gloria fumbled inside her purse and pulled out her cell phone. She dialed Andrea's cell phone and the call went to voice mail so she tapped out a text message, '*Please call me right away. Alice and Brian have been trying to reach you since yesterday.*'

Alice motioned Gloria to follow her to the kitchen. "Would you like some coffee? I'll make a pot?" She flitted back and forth across the kitchen as she started a fresh pot of coffee, rambling the entire time. "Andrea's parents, the Thorntons, they always call me back and also Andrea."

The coffee finished brewing and Alice poured two cups. She set one of the cups in front of Gloria. "I make a fresh batch of churros. You try one?" Alice placed a basket of deep fried, sugarcoated sticks next to Gloria's coffee.

"Thank you. I've never had one." Gloria absentmindedly reached for one and bit the end. "These are delicious."

"I make samples for Brian and Andrea's engagement party." Tears filled Alice's eyes. "But maybe I no need now." Alice clasped her hands. "You think I have to move back to New York?" she asked.

"I hope not." Gloria set the churro on a napkin and squeezed Alice's hand. "We'll get this straightened out. Don't worry."

The women chatted for several moments as Gloria attempted to ease Alice's mind, all the while wondering what was going on in Nantucket.

"Perhaps her cell phone died and she needs to charge it. You know how forgetful these young people are about charging their cell phones."

"I...maybe you're right. I hope so," Alice said.

"The reason I stopped by is because Andrea is threatening to break off the engagement so we...all of the Garden Girls, as well as Brian and Paul, have decided to drive to Nantucket to talk some sense into Andrea. I'm here to ask if you'd like to go with us. You're like a mother to Andrea and she loves you. Maybe she'll listen to you, if no one else."

"I dunno. Andrea, she stubborn." Alice shook her head. "What if she not come back?"

"As least we can say we tried." Gloria finished her second churro, downed the last of her coffee and reached for her purse. "We're leaving at 6:00 a.m. Monday morning. Do you want to go with us?"

"Si." Alice nodded. "I hope Miss Andrea is okay."

Gloria's cell phone chirped. She reached inside her purse and pulled out her phone. It was Margaret.

"Hello?"

"I hope you're sitting down," were the first words out of Margaret's mouth.

The tone of Margaret's voice caused Gloria to do just that. She eased back onto the barstool she'd just vacated. "I'm sitting."

"I was doing some research, checking out the ferries that travel from the mainland to Nantucket and I ran across an article in the Nantucket Morning News from this morning."

A chill ran down Gloria's spine. Margaret was about to drop a bomb.

"I'll read you the headline on the front page," Margaret said. "Former New York socialite, Andrea Thornton Malone, has mysteriously vanished from the island of Nantucket while vacationing with her parents, David Thornton and Dr. Libby Casteel-Thornton."

Chapter 3

"You're kidding," Gloria said.

"Check it out yourself. I won't go into detail, just to say Andrea and an unnamed friend visited the local farmer's market yesterday morning. They became separated when Andrea told the unnamed man she needed to use the restroom and she never returned."

Margaret continued. "From what the paper said, police and local volunteers have torn the island apart and they can't find her...or her body."

Gloria pressed two fingers to her temple and shot Alice, who stood nearby, a guarded look. "I'm going to check it out now. I'll call you back." Gloria hung up and turned to Alice. "There may be a reason Andrea isn't answering your calls. We need to log onto the internet."

The women hurried to Andrea's library and over to her desk where Alice settled into the chair and turned the computer on. "What is going on Miss Gloria? You're white as a ghost."

"I'll tell you in a minute," Gloria said, her mind reeling at Margaret's discovery.

After the computer fired up, the women switched places and Gloria opened a search screen, typed *Nantucket Morning News* in the search bar and then clicked on the icon.

Both women leaned in and read the article Margaret described. It was brief and to the point. Andrea had gone to the farmer's market the previous morning with an unnamed friend and then vanished into thin air.

According to the story, authorities had questioned David and Libby Thornton, Andrea's parents, as well as the unnamed person, who was the last person seen with Andrea.

The article finished by saying so far, no other details about the case had been released and authorities were not divulging information about the case to the public.

"Miss Andrea is missing." A stunned Alice dropped into a nearby chair and clutched her chest. "We need to go there Miss Gloria." She turned wild eyes to Gloria.

"We will, Alice, just as soon as we can cobble this trip together." Gloria shot out of the chair and hurried around the side of the desk. She gently hugged the woman. "Don't worry, Alice. We'll get to the bottom of this," Gloria vowed. *Hopefully before it's too late* she silently added.

***

"I can't go." Ruth stood on Gloria's back porch and kicked at a leaf that had blown into the corner. "It's late and no one from the district branch has approved the time off." Her shoulders drooped. "I even sent in a backup for LWOP, just in case."

Gloria shifted to the side and gazed out into the yard. She watched Mally patrol the perimeter of the garden. "What is LWOP?"

"Leave without pay."

"Are you saying you don't have vacation time?" Gloria asked.

"Yeah, I've got plenty. The only time I've taken off this year was for our cruise," Ruth said. "I could always call in sick."

"We might be gone for several days." Gloria didn't think it sounded like a good plan. "Can't you call someone else? Surely after all these years they will understand you have a family emergency."

If Ruth couldn't get the time off, it would throw a wrench into their cross-country road trip. There was no way nine adults could fit in one vehicle. At best, Annabelle could comfortably carry four people. Five would be tight.

Dot owned a van, but Ray used it for transporting restaurant supplies. Margaret drove a newer SUV but even that would be tight.

"I'll try again, but no one in management typically works this late in the day." Ruth turned to go. "I was so excited about this trip."

Gloria watched as her friend shuffled to her newly renovated van and climbed inside.

Paul was waiting in the kitchen when Gloria made her way back inside. "Judging by the look on Ruth's face, she had some bad news," he guessed.

"Yeah. She hasn't gotten approval for time off from the post office so she doesn't think she'll be able to make the trip."

Mally, Gloria's springer Spaniel, padded over and nudged her hand with her snout. Gloria absentmindedly patted her head. "Are you sure

Allie won't mind taking care of Mally and Puddles while we're gone?"

Allie was Paul's youngest child. She had moved back to Belhaven from the Detroit area a short time ago and was living in Paul's farmhouse until she could get back on her feet, which wouldn't be long since she'd recently been hired by the Montbay County Sheriff's station working as a dispatcher.

"Nope. I think she'll enjoy the company," Paul said. Gloria knew Paul worried about Allie, living all alone out in the middle of nowhere in the big old farmhouse. Mally loved everyone and wouldn't harm a flea, she was a good watchdog and would alert Allie if anyone tried to come to the door.

"I'm so worried about Andrea," Gloria confessed to her husband. "Do you think she ran away?"

Paul, a former Montbay County Sheriff, had seen it all. It was not unheard of for someone to become overwhelmed by their circumstances and just up and disappear. More often than not, they would eventually return home although, to him, Andrea didn't seem to be the "flighty" type."

"I don't know, Gloria. We won't know until we get there." Paul wandered over to the door and grabbed the keys to the garage. "I'm going to head out to the shop to finish my fall planter box. I'd like to get it done before we leave Monday." Paul had set up a small workshop in the back of the garage for his woodworking projects.

He bent down and planted a kiss on his bride's cheek. "Try not to worry. I think she'll turn up. She probably just needed to get away."

"I have a feeling her parents were pressuring her to move back to New York," Gloria said.

"There's not much we can do from here. We'll have to wait until we get there." He wandered down the steps and disappeared from sight. Mally trotted after him.

Gloria poured a glass of lemonade before she picked up her cell phone a second time. She dialed Dot's cell phone and a breathless Dot finally answered. "Hi Gloria."

"Hi Dot. Sorry to bother you." Gloria glanced at the wall clock. "You sound busy."

"No problem. What's up?"

Gloria briefly explained how Margaret had stumbled upon the Nantucket local news and discovered Andrea had disappeared. "Ruth was just here. She doesn't think she can make the trip because she hasn't gotten approval for the time off."

"I heard. She stopped by here, too, threatening to call in sick if they refuse to give her the time off. She said she already cleared it with Kenny and even contacted her part-time replacement, Mary, who said she'd be happy to cover for her."

"We need a backup plan," Gloria said. "Do you think Ray and Johnnie can get by if you drive the van?"

"Yeah, we already talked about it but you know I don't like driving long distances," Dot said.

"Maybe Rose could drive," Gloria suggested.

"No way! I want to get there in one piece and Rose is a maniac behind the wheel." Somehow, that tidbit of information didn't surprise Gloria. Rose was a real firecracker.

"Maybe Brian can drive."

They discussed the possibilities of who might work best as a second designated driver and finally decided if push came to shove and Ruth wasn't able to make the trip, they would ask Margaret.

Gloria kept her cell phone close the rest of the day as she washed several loads of laundry and pulled her suitcases from the spare bedroom upstairs to begin packing for the trip. She'd never been to Nantucket or even the State of Massachusetts and decided a little research into the summer weather and temperatures was in order.

She headed to the dining room and settled in front of the computer. Puddles, Gloria's cat, leapt onto Gloria's lap, circled several times and then curled up to take a nap.

Gloria absentmindedly stroked Puddles' head as she studied the weather. "At least the weather looks good," she told her sleeping cat. "Highs in the 70's, lows in the 50's." She would need a little of everything...shorts, t-shirts, sweatshirts and maybe even a sweater.

Gloria checked her email, balanced her checkbook and finally shut the computer off when the dryer beeped. She scooped Puddles into her arms, holding him close as she carried him into the living room to set him in her recliner, one of his favorite napping spots.

The afternoon flew by and the more time that passed, the more certain Gloria became that not hearing from Ruth meant bad news. She had suggested to Ruth several times it might be time to retire or even cut back on working full time at the post office.

She had a feeling Ruth didn't need the money, but working gave her a sense of purpose. Ruth loved chatting with the Belhaven locals. It was the perfect job for Ruth. She loved to gossip. People loved to talk.

Gloria folded several pairs of blue jeans and carefully packed them in her half of the suitcase. She added a couple thick fluffy sweaters, a hoodie, plus a pair of capris and lightweight V-neck shirts.

When she finished, she realized she wasn't even close to finishing her packing and her clothes were already creeping onto Paul's half. There was no way around it. He would need his own suitcase.

She flipped the top, zipped the cover and then dragged it over to the side of the dresser. Mally darted into the bedroom and tromped over the top of the suitcase before flopping down on the floor. "You're done working in the workshop?" she asked her pooch.

Gloria finished folding her laundry and then wandered into the kitchen to check on dinner. She dug out her crockpot and decided to throw together a slow cooker chicken dinner. They still had a surplus of vegetables from the previous summer's garden and she wanted to use up as many of the vegetables as possible before harvesting this year's garden.

Gloria had given away many of the fruits and vegetables from her bountiful garden to the area shut-ins they visited every Sunday afternoon. It seemed that this year, the list of elderly and homebound had grown. What had once taken the girls a couple hours on a Sunday afternoon, now took all afternoon and they weren't finished with their rounds until early evening.

The women were tossing around the idea of splitting the list with half visiting one group and the other half visiting the other. Divide and conquer. It was a rewarding volunteer project and Gloria wasn't sure who enjoyed it more…the shut-ins, or the group of friends who made the rounds.

One of the locals, Shirley Jackson, had fallen in her bathroom the previous Saturday and been unable to crawl to the phone. If it hadn't been for the girls visiting after church the following day, who knew how long she would have lain there, waiting for someone to find her.

Gloria lifted the lid and waited for the burst of steam and heat to escape before she peered inside. The aroma of rosemary and simmering chicken wafted up. She reached for the fork sitting next to the crockpot and stabbed the chicken. The meat easily peeled off and she pulled a small piece out for the chef's taste-test.

The moist meat melted in her mouth. Gloria reached inside the silverware drawer for a clean fork and then stuck the fork in the carrots and potatoes. The vegetables were tender so she shut the crockpot off, replaced the lid and headed to the workshop.

She was halfway across the sidewalk when the sound of tires squealing on the asphalt out front stopped her in her tracks.

Ruth's van careened into the driveway and came to a screeching halt. She flung the door open and darted across the drive. "I finally heard back from the boss!"

Chapter 4

"What's the verdict?" Gloria asked. "Yea or nay?"

"A big fat yea!" Ruth said breathlessly. "It took a little strong arming on my end, but Devlin finally caved and approved a whole week off."

"That's great news," Gloria said. She shifted her gaze and glanced at the workshop. "I was just getting ready to call Paul in for dinner. I made a crockpot chicken and vegetables. We have plenty. Would you like to join us?"

"I should go home and start packing," Ruth said. "I still have a few more gadgets I want to set up inside the van before we hit the road."

"You have all weekend," Gloria pointed out. "We're not leaving until Monday morning."

"I guess you're right. I don't want to impose."

Gloria flung an arm around Ruth's shoulder. "You're not imposing. We'd love to have you eat with us. Let me go get Paul. He's in the workshop."

Ruth wandered to the porch to wait while Gloria headed to the workshop. The buzz of Paul's sander and the smell of sawdust filled the room. She didn't want to scare Paul so she waited until the sanding stopped. "Dinner is ready."

Paul flinched and spun around. "You scared me half to death."

"Sorry," Gloria apologized. "That's exactly what I was trying not to do. It's getting late and dinner is ready."

Paul pulled off his safety glasses and set them next to the sander before unplugging it. "I can finish this tomorrow." He wiped the back of his hands on the front of his blue jeans. "I can't wait to try this chicken you've been raving about."

Gloria reached for the doorknob. "Ruth stopped by to tell me she got the time off next week so I invited her to stay for dinner."

"I'm sure you made plenty." Paul rubbed his wife's shoulder as they wandered out of the workshop. "I can't wait to see her van."

Gloria had told Paul about Ruth's latest additions to her van and since he was a retired sheriff who was familiar with state-of-the-art vehicle gizmos and gadgets, he couldn't wait to see what she'd done.

The fact a bulletproof armor company had teamed up with Ruth to test the new material had piqued Paul's interest, not to mention the fact Ruth had a reputation for spy, surveillance and high tech investigative gear.

"We'll eat first," Gloria said as she closed the shop door behind them.

"Hi Ruth." Paul greeted Gloria's friend, who was pacing back and forth across the porch.

"Hi Paul," Ruth said. "I hope I'm not imposing."

"Not at all." He smiled at Ruth and turned to Gloria. "Any news from Andrea?"

"No." Gloria's shoulders slumped. "I tried calling a couple more times but the calls are still going right to her voice mail."

She went on. "Maybe we should leave earlier than Monday."

"It will be tough rounding up all the troops on such short notice," Paul pointed out. He held the door for Ruth and Gloria before heading to the kitchen sink. "I heard you have a new and improved ride. I can't wait to take a look at it after we eat."

Ruth clasped her hands. "I can't wait to try it out next week. You should see the polycarbonate on the windows. You can't even tell that it's bullet-resistant." She proceeded to talk technical surveillance lingo with Paul while Gloria set the table.

Gloria had baked a cherry cream cheese surprise pie earlier that day, using a batch of fresh-frozen cherries from the previous year's harvest that she'd found hidden in the bottom of her deep freeze.

Michigan cherries were still a few weeks out before being ready to pick, and Gloria and Paul had discussed taking a weekend trip to the Traverse City area to pick their own. The trip might be on hold now that they were heading to Nantucket.

Ruth stopped chatting about her van long enough to help Gloria finish setting the table while Paul headed to the bathroom.

When he returned, he eased into the seat at the head of the table while Gloria sat next to him. Ruth sat at the other end.

The trio bowed their heads while Paul prayed. "Dear Heavenly Father, thank you for this wonderful meal before us. Lord, we thank you for this day, for blessing us with a beautiful summer season. We also say a special prayer for our friend, Andrea. We pray she's safe and sound and just needs some time to herself. In Jesus name we pray, amen."

"Amen," Gloria and Ruth echoed.

"Guests first." Gloria motioned to the platter of chicken and the heaping bowls filled with cooked carrots and potatoes.

"Oh, I forgot the dinner rolls." Gloria scooted her chair back and hurried to the pantry where she pulled out an unopened package of dinner rolls. "Sorry, these aren't made from scratch." She removed the twist tie and set the package of rolls on the table.

"I'm sure they're delicious." Ruth eased a chicken thigh onto her plate and passed the dish to her friend. "This is a real treat, Gloria. I hardly ever cook a meal from scratch since it's only me. I typically throw together a sandwich or pop a frozen dinner in the microwave."

A wave of guilt washed over Gloria. Ruth was single and lived by herself, which meant she ate the majority of her meals alone.

Gloria didn't know how to respond and knew Ruth wasn't trying to make her feel guilty. She was simply stating a fact. "I-I'll send some leftovers home." She placed a piece of chicken onto her plate and passed the meat to Paul. She added a scoop of carrots and potatoes and then slid a roll next to the chicken.

The chicken was as tender and delicious as the sample she'd tasted earlier and Gloria was glad she'd made a big pot.

The conversation flowed easily as they discussed the upcoming trip, Paul and Gloria's thriving garden and MIA Andrea.

"She's probably hiding from her parents." Ruth tore a chunk off her roll and chewed thoughtfully. "The girl's pride is wounded. She'll come around."

"When we find her, we'll drag her home," Gloria joked. "But seriously, if we get there and she insists she doesn't want to return to Belhaven, we can't force her. It has to be her decision."

After they finished eating, Paul cleared the table while Gloria grabbed dessert plates and the homemade cherry dessert. She set the dishes and dessert on the table and headed to the freezer for a pint of vanilla ice cream.

She cut three large pieces of pie and passed them around the table. Paul scooped a spoonful of ice cream and handed the carton to Gloria. She shook her head. "No ice cream for me. I like my cherry pie plain."

She handed the carton to Ruth, who carefully eased two large spoonfuls of ice cream next to her pie. "I love vanilla ice cream. Vanilla bean is the best." She sawed off the tip of the pie, added a large chunk of ice cream and popped it into her mouth. "This is delicious. It has the perfect ratio of tart and sweet. I never was good at making homemade cherry pie. My crust always turns out too crumbly. What's in it?"

"I made the crust from scratch and layered it with cream cheese, cinnamon sugar, covered it with some cherries I found in my freezer and then topped it with a layer of cinnamon crumble." Gloria cut off a chunk for her first taste. "Mmm. It is good. I think the layer of cream cheese was a nice addition. I have to admit this recipe isn't for the faint of heart. It took a long time to throw together."

"Then I feel special to have gotten a chance to try it." Ruth reached for another spoon full. "How is the trip planning progressing?"

"I have no idea. The only thing I've done is take a look at the weather and a quick glimpse at local hotels. I need to check with Margaret to see if she was able to find accommodations for the nine of us in Nantucket." From what little Gloria was able to glean online, the island was small and lodging limited…and pricey.

Since Paul, Gloria and Ruth were the drivers, they discussed logistics, drive time and who would ride in each of the vehicles. It was decided Lucy and Brian would ride with Paul and Gloria. Ruth could easily take Margaret, Dot, Alice and Rose in her van.

Ruth scraped the last piece of piecrust off her plate and popped it into her mouth. "Do you think it's wise to have Alice and Rose riding in the same vehicle?"

Gloria frowned. She hadn't thought about that. Alice and Rose had started off on the wrong foot and, although they had reached an uneasy truce, perhaps riding in the same vehicle might be pressing their luck. "You're right. I'll give you Lucy and you give me Alice so we don't have to separate Rose and Dot."

After they finished their dessert, Gloria shooed Paul and Ruth outside to check out her van before it got dark while she loaded the dishwasher and assembled a to-go plate for Ruth.

She met them in the driveway a short time later with the container of food in hand. Gloria handed the grocery bag and container to Ruth. "I put your food in a Styrofoam container so there's no need to return the dish."

Ruth opened the bag and looked inside. "I hope this doesn't leak on my seat. I just had them cleaned." She opened the driver's side door, leaned in and set the bag on the passenger seat. "Well, at least I don't have far to go. I'm sure it will be fine."

Paul's cell phone began ringing and he excused himself. "It's Allie." He headed toward the porch.

Gloria faced Ruth. "We should plan a pre-trip meeting Sunday after church and before we make our rounds so we can go over the final details."

"Sounds good." Ruth gave Gloria a thumbs up before she climbed into the driver's seat and pulled the door shut. She rolled down the window. "Thanks again for dinner. It was delicious." She shifted her gaze and glanced at Paul, who was standing on the porch staring at his cell phone. "Maybe someday I'll get lucky and find a catch like Paul."

She didn't wait for a reply as she started the van, revved the engine and backed out of the drive before pulling onto the road.

Gloria didn't have time to dwell on the comment. Paul leapt off the porch steps and began running across the drive. "Allie's been in a car accident!"

Chapter 5

A bolt of fear shot down Gloria's spine. "I-is she okay?"

"She sent a text and told me she's banged up. She's at Green Springs Memorial Hospital." Paul ran a frazzled hand though his hair.

"I'll go get the car keys." Gloria hurried into the house, grabbed the keys, her purse and cell phone before dashing out the door, locking it behind her.

Paul absentmindedly climbed into the passenger side of the car while Gloria slid behind the wheel. It was a short, quiet drive to the hospital while Paul worried and Gloria prayed.

She dropped her husband off at the emergency room entrance and drove to the parking lot in search of a parking spot.

Paul was nowhere in sight when Gloria reached the waiting room. She approached the desk. "My husband came in here looking for his daughter, Allison Kennedy. She was involved in a car accident."

The nurse directed Gloria down the hall, which looked all too familiar. It was the same emergency room where Brian had been admitted after being attacked.

Nurses at a second nurse's station inside the emergency room corridor directed Gloria to a small waiting room where she found her husband standing by the window.

"The woman at the front desk said she's in surgery but won't tell me her current condition." Paul's eyes filled with unshed tears. "She said I'll have to wait until the doctor comes out."

It was a tense hour and a half while the two waited for some word on Allie's condition. The fact that she'd been able to send a brief text to her father after the accident gave Gloria hope it wasn't too bad, although the unsettling news that she was in "surgery" did nothing to ease Paul and Gloria's minds.

Finally, a man wearing green scrubs strode into the waiting room, his eyes scanning the room.

Paul made his way over and Gloria followed behind. "Mr. Kennedy?"

"Yes, I'm Allison Kennedy's father."

"I'm Doctor Cole, the surgeon who operated on your daughter. Allison is going to be okay."

Gloria let out the breath she'd been holding and clasped her throat. "Thank you Jesus."

The doctor went on to tell them she'd been involved in a front end collision, which drove the steering wheel into her arm. A team of surgeons had placed several pins in her arm and it would take some time for Allie to heal.

"We're going to keep her overnight to monitor her condition and then take another look at her tomorrow morning," the doctor told them. "She's settled into her hospital room. I can take you there if you'd like to see her."

The trio strode across the waiting room and down the long, sterile corridor. Dr. Cole stopped in front of a door, not far from the nurse's station.

"Allie, you have company," the doctor said as he slid the privacy curtain to the side and stepped to the end of the bed.

Allie, who had been staring out the window, turned.

Gloria's heart sank at the sight of the young woman's bruised forehead and bandaged arm. She looked so small and frail lying in the bed.

Paul slowly walked to the side and leaned over the edge of the bed. Gloria couldn't hear the murmured conversation but when Paul stood, Allie attempted a small smile.

The doctor exited the room after promising to return in the morning to check on her. Paul and Gloria stayed by Allie's side for most of the evening, until they were sure Allie was going to be all right. The nurses came by to monitor her condition, check her vitals and to give her another dose of pain medication.

Allie drifted in and out of sleep and finally, during one of her periods of being awake, Paul stood. "You get some rest and we'll be back first thing tomorrow morning." He gently kissed his daughter's forehead before he and Gloria tiptoed out of the room as Allie drifted off to sleep again.

It was the wee hours of the morning by the time the couple stumbled through the back porch door. After they climbed into bed, Paul and Gloria joined hands and prayed for Allie, for all their children before Gloria drifted off into a dreamless sleep.

Paul, who had tossed and turned all night, woke first and crawled out of bed. She could hear him in the kitchen, talking to Allie on the phone.

Gloria slipped her bathrobe on and wandered into the kitchen. "...we'll be along around eleven then." There was a small pause. "I love you too, Allie." Paul pressed the button on the cell phone and set it on the kitchen table. "The doctor was in early to check on her. She's sore and stiff and the nurses gave her something for the aches and pains, not to mention her arm, but other than that, they're going to release her."

Gloria headed to the coffee pot. "I'll whip up a quick breakfast and then we can ride to the hospital together," she offered.

Breakfast consisted of fried sausage patties, diced fried potatoes, scrambled eggs and toast. "I don't think I should make the trip to Nantucket." Paul reached for his slice of toast.

"I won't go either." Gloria grabbed the shaker of salt. She sprinkled some on top of her eggs and fried potatoes. “The others can make the trip without me.”

Paul gave his wife a quick glance. “I think you should still go. Allie will be fine, but I would feel better if I stayed home and kept an eye on her. Not only that, but I don’t want to have to leave Mally and Puddles with her. She’s going to be stiff and sore for several days.”

Gloria was on the fence. On the one hand, she felt guilty about making the trip knowing Paul was at home with an injured daughter while she was gallivanting halfway across the country. “I’ll think about it,” Gloria finally said.

The two of them finished their breakfast and headed to the car. They swung by Paul’s farm on the way to the hospital to fill a backpack with clean clothes for Allie before heading to the hospital.

When they reached the hospital, Allie was sitting in the chair by the window, still wearing her hospital gown. “I had to trash the clothes I was wearing. They're a mess." She pointed to the tray next to her hospital bed. "All I need to do is fill these out and I'm free to leave."

Paul helped her fill out the forms since her broken arm was also her writing arm.

After they finished the paperwork, Gloria carried Allie's backpack to the small bathroom. She waited while Allie limped inside before easing the backpack onto the bathroom floor. "Let me know if you need help, dear," Gloria said as she closed the bathroom door.

Allie was in there for a long time and Gloria was about to head to the small room to check on her when she emerged, her expression pinched and her face pale. "I think I need another pain killer," she grimaced.

A hospital worker stopped by a short time later to inspect the release forms. After inspecting the forms, she handed a small packet of papers to Paul. "There are several prescriptions here. You can stop by the hospital pharmacy on your way out to have them filled."

"I'll run downstairs, get the prescription filled and meet you in the lobby," Gloria said. Paul handed her the papers and she hurried from the room. Thankfully, the pharmacy wasn't busy and it didn't take the staff long to fill the prescriptions.

Gloria paid for the medication and then made her way to the emergency room exit where Paul and Allie, who was seated in a wheelchair, waited by the door.

"I'll go get the car," Gloria said. She hurried to the parking lot to pull the car around while Paul waited with Allie.

After easing Allie into the back seat, Paul climbed in next to her. During the ride back to the farm, Allie filled them in on the accident. She told them she'd been driving home from her new job at the sheriff's department when a carload of teenagers attempted to pass her in a no passing zone.

There had been a small hill, and another car had been coming from the opposite direction. Allie had jerked the steering wheel to avoid a collision, drove into a ditch, up an embankment and hit a tree. Thankfully, she hadn't been going fast, but still fast enough to total her car and break her arm.

Halfway home, she nodded off in the back seat and didn't wake until they arrived at the farm. Allie didn't even put up a fuss when they told her they wanted her to stay with them for a few days, until she was back on her feet.

Paul helped her settle into the downstairs spare bedroom and closed the door after assuring himself she was as comfortable as possible.

Gloria was in the kitchen reading the morning newspaper when he walked in. She peered at him over the top of her reading glasses. "I think I should stay home."

"I think you should go." Paul pulled out the chair next to her and eased into the seat. "I asked Allie and she thinks you should go, too. You need to find Andrea and bring her home."

"You're trying to get rid of me," Gloria said.

"No, I'm not, but I would like to keep an eye on Allie." Paul shook his head. "There's no reason for both of us to hover over her. In a day or so, she'll be climbing the walls, anxious to get out of here and then what?"

Paul had a point. There was no sense in having both of them hang around the house. "I feel bad about leaving you."

"There's no reason to feel bad." Paul leaned over and kissed his wife. "I'll hold down the fort and you'll be back before you know it."

Gloria sucked in a breath. "If you're sure…"

"I'm sure."

"I guess I better finish packing."

Chapter 6

If Gloria could sum up the drive from Belhaven to Hyannis, Massachusetts, it would be in a single phrase…pedal to the metal. Ruth had one mission in mind…to arrive in the coastal town of Hyannis as quickly as possible.

Since Paul had decided not to take the trip, Brian, Lucy and Alice rode with Gloria while Margaret, Dot and Rose rode with Ruth.

The fourteen plus hour drive, which included a couple quick gas, food and bathroom breaks, caused them to arrive in town not long after the last ferry carrying passengers to Nantucket had already departed.

Margaret, bless her heart, had made all of the arrangements before they hit the road. She had calculated the length of the long drive, guessing they wouldn't make it in time to catch the last ferry to Nantucket, so she found a small mom 'n pop motel near the harbor where they spent the night.

Brian opted for a room to himself and Gloria had to wonder if after the long day, surrounded by women, he needed a break from them. He had been a good sport the entire ride and even offered to drive part of the way, but Gloria was concerned it would give him a headache so she decided she would drive the entire distance.

Annabelle's new engine ran like a top. The ride was smooth and, except for driving at or over the posted speed limits most of the time because of speed demon Ruth, it was uneventful.

At one point during the trip, she caught a glimpse of Brian, huddled in the corner of the backseat working on something with his hands. When she tried to ask him what he was doing, he hurriedly dropped it into the backpack he'd brought with him and placed it on the floor of the car.

Margaret had pre-purchased the ferry tickets as well as reserved a parking spot for Annabelle in the ferry's parking lot.

The group determined they would need a vehicle to get around the island so Ruth offered to take her van over on the car ferry.

Check in was quick and uneventful, and before turning in for the night, Gloria called Paul to check on Allie. Paul reassured her that although he could tell Allie was still in a lot of pain, she seemed to be improving.

Gloria, Lucy and Alice shared one room. There were two beds and a rollaway. The women drew straws and Gloria came up on the short end of the stick. Lucy took one of the full-size beds while Alice got the other. Gloria got the rollaway.

The narrow rollaway creaked under Gloria's weight but she barely noticed. She flopped down on the bed and was out like a light.

***

Bright sun shone in through the curtains early the next morning. Alice, who was already up, emerged from the bathroom while Gloria was searching the small counter for the in-room coffee pot. "Coffee. I need coffee."

"The coffee pot is over there. I go across the street to the coffee shop and buy good stuff," Alice announced. She wrinkled her nose as she pointed at the pot. "This stuff, it not good."

Alice hurried out the door while Gloria headed to the bathroom. When Alice returned, she was juggling a to-go coffee holder and four cups, along with a brown paper bag filled with breakfast sandwiches.

Brian held the door and followed her in. "Look what I found on my way back," Alice joked. "I tell the girls next door about the coffee shop, too."

They settled in at the table while Lucy headed to the bathroom to get dressed. Alice lifted the lid on her coffee and dumped a liquid creamer inside. "It going to be a long day."

"I'm sure it will." Gloria sipped her coffee and wondered where to begin their search for Andrea. Perhaps she had hopped the ferry and headed back to the mainland. If that were the case, they'd never find her.

After they finished their coffee and breakfast sandwiches, Gloria glanced at her watch. "It's time to head over to the ferry."

They hurriedly packed their bags and met the others near the back of Ruth's van. Brian tossed the bags inside the back before everyone climbed into the vehicles for the short trip to the ferry dock.

Gloria pulled into the lot and the first empty spot she found. Brian, Alice, Lucy and Gloria exited the car and hurried to the boarding area to join the others while Ruth eased her van to the end of the long line of vehicles waiting to be loaded onto the ferry.

When Ruth got to the front of the line, she slid out of the driver's seat and eyed the attendant. She handed him some folded bills. "There's more where this came from if you make sure my baby isn't dinged during the trip." She patted the side of the van.

The man shoved the money in his pocket and climbed behind the wheel. "Yes ma'am."

Ruth watched him like a hawk as he drove her van onto the car ferry and disappeared from sight.

Lucy wandered over to join Ruth. She shaded her eyes and gazed into the bowels of the ship. "It's supposed to be bullet proof. I would think that would also make it scratch, dent and ding proof."

"I'm not taking any chances," Ruth replied.

"So I guess me shooting at it is out of the question."

Ruth shook her head violently. "No way Jose."

The group gathered near the gangway and boarded the ferry. Margaret led the way and they settled into a row of seats near the center of the boat.

"I'll be right back." Ruth walked to the rear of the ferry and exited through a double set of doors.

She returned a short time later and Gloria slid over to make room for her on the bench seat. "Where did you wander off to?"

"I wanted to check on the van," Ruth said. "Remind me to head below deck to the vehicle holding area before we dock so I can keep an eye on the attendants."

Gloria lifted her hand in a small salute. "Will do." She shifted her attention to the window. Now that it was daylight, she was able to get a good look at the picturesque town of Hyannis.

Margaret, who sat on Gloria's other side, gazed out the window. "I hear Nantucket is equally as lovely."

Despite the reason for the visit, Gloria was looking forward to seeing the island. She hoped that once they tracked Andrea down, they would have time to explore. Gloria felt in her bones Andrea was alive, that she had just taken a break from everything and everyone, and once Brian and Andrea were reunited, they would be able to work things out.

Gloria had no idea Brian and Andrea's reunion was going to be the least of her worries.

***

The boat ride flew by as the group discussed the strategy for tracking down Andrea.

Gloria had managed to track down the name of the hotel where Andrea and her parents were staying. She pulled her cell phone from her purse and switched it on. "Andrea and her parents are staying at Ocean View Resort on Breeze Boulevard. According to the hotel description, it's close to town and a short walk to the beaches."

She turned to Margaret, the unofficial travel planner. "What's the name of the place where we're staying?"

Margaret reached into her purse and pulled out a sheet of paper. "We're staying at Craggy Manor Inn. The woman I spoke to on the phone said we're only a ten minute bike ride to the beach."

"Bike ride, as in pedal bike?" Rose snorted. "I ain't been on a bike since I was a young 'un."

"Me either," Gloria agreed. "There's no way we're all going to be able to ride in Ruth's van at the same time. We need to split up into groups to search for Andrea, some by foot, some by bike and the rest by van."

The ferry began to slow. Ruth bolted from her seat and disappeared through the back door.

Gloria waited until she was out of sight before turning to the others. "We can all squeeze into the van for the short ride to Andrea's hotel and our hotel. Later, we'll look into renting bikes."

"What about a scooter?" Lucy asked. "I'd try a scooter."

The ferry docked a short time later. The group exited the ferry and found their luggage piled on a cart near the gangway. Off in the distance, Gloria could see Ruth, who was sitting in her van near the loading zone.

The group dragged their suitcases to the end of the dock and around the back of the van. After some finagling, they managed to stack all but one of the suitcases in the back. Gloria offered to hold it in the front passenger seat for the short ride.

During the drive, Gloria phoned Andrea, hoping against hope she would hear her bright cheery voice on the other end. The call went to voice mail.

"Brian, you need to contact the Thorntons to see if they will give you any clues as to what happened to Andrea."

"I don't think they'll talk," he said as he turned to Alice. "If they won't talk to me, maybe they'll talk to you."

"You try first. This is your woman," Alice said. "She expect her knight in shining armor."

"To arrive on scene in a bulletproof van," Gloria teased.

Ruth drove the van under the portico of the Ocean View Resort and shifted to park while Brian slid the side door open and stepped onto the paved drive. "Keep your phones on. I'll call you as soon as I have some news."

The girls all wished Brian luck. They watched him stroll through the sliding glass doors and disappear inside the massive resort lobby.

Alice slid the door closed. "We've done all we can. Now all we can do is pray and wait."

Ruth punched their motel's address into her GPS and drove out of the hotel parking lot and onto the street. Once again, Gloria was impressed by Margaret's travel savvy. "Have you thought about becoming a travel consultant?"

"I've booked so many trips." Margaret shook her head. "Course Don and I don't travel as much anymore. He would rather stay home and golf with his buddies."

Ruth's GPS led them right to their motel. Gloria leaned forward to catch her first glimpse. It didn't look nearly as swanky as the one Andrea and her family were staying in, but it was cute and quaint, and Gloria was certain it would be perfect.

Margaret had managed to book three suites, all side by side. Check in was quick and easy and the clerk even let them check in early without charging extra.

The exterior of the motel was deceiving. Their suites were large and spacious. Near the back of the motel was a meticulously landscaped center courtyard. There was also a swimming pool with lounge chairs around the pool.

Each of the suites contained a separate bedroom area with two queen beds. There was an efficiency kitchen and compact living room, complete with a sleeper sofa.

Gloria offered to bunk with Brian while Dot, Ruth and Rose took one suite and Margaret, Lucy and Alice took the other.

She quickly unpacked her clothes, placing them inside the right hand dresser drawers. She left the left hand side empty for Brian.

She had finished arranging her toiletries in the spacious bathroom when her cell phone began ringing. It was Brian. Gloria whispered a small prayer before hitting the answer button.

"I hope you have good news," Gloria said.

"I wish I did." Brian's voice echoed on the other end. "I caught up with Andrea's parents and confronted them. They told me I might as well turn right around and head back to Belhaven because they weren't going to tell me anything."

There was an edge to Brian's voice as he continued. "I did find out one thing...the name of the person Andrea was with at the time of her disappearance."

"Who was it?"

"It was Andrea's ex-boyfriend. His name is Sean Brodwell."

Chapter 7

Gloria loosened her grip on the phone and it almost slipped from her grasp. “I hope I heard you wrong. Did you say Andrea was with an ex-boyfriend when she went missing?”

“Yep,” Brian said grimly. “I’m heading to the farmer’s market, the last place Andrea was seen. It’s not far from here. I’ll call you back.”

The line disconnected and Gloria frowned at the phone. She hadn’t envisioned things turning out this way and her heart sank. She hoped there was some mistake. She couldn’t imagine Andrea being so fickle and hooking up with an ex-boyfriend. Technically, Brian and Andrea were still engaged!

She hurried to the other suites and quickly told the girls what Brian had said.

Ruth unzipped her backpack and plugged her computer in. "We need to figure out where this farmer's market is located."

"We also need to track down Sean Brodwell," Dot said. "What if Brian hunts the man down and the two get into a physical altercation?" The last thing Brian needed was to get into a knockdown, drag out brawl with a fresh head injury, not to mention the prospect of being arrested.

"You're right."

Ruth quickly located the farmer's market. "It's at the entrance to Land's End Lighthouse."

The women darted to the van and climbed in.

Ruth flipped the GPS on and did a quick search for points of interest. "Got it." She started the van, shoved it into drive and peeled out of the parking lot, tires squealing.

They sped down the side streets, taking the backroads to the location and arrived a short time later.

Gloria flung the side door open and leapt from the van before Ruth had time to shift into park. The farmer's market was closed, the booths shuttered. Off in the distance was a small lighthouse. Several people were wandering along the shoreline.

There was one lone figure strolling along the sandy beach. It was Brian.

The other women exited the van and hurried after Gloria.

"We're going to help search the area," an out of breath Gloria told Brian when she caught up to him.

Brian stopped abruptly and swung around. "Maybe we should go back home." His jaw tightened. "If she wants this other man, Sean, she can have him. I don't want to waste my time, begging someone to come back who doesn't want me."

Gloria tugged on Brian's arm. "The news is shocking, but it doesn't mean we should jump to conclusions. We don't know the whole story."

"You can head back to the motel," Brian said. "I'm going to stop by Andrea's hotel to see if I can find out if her *friend,* Sean, is staying there, too. I'd like to have a chat with him."

The tone of Brian's voice sent warning bells off in Gloria's head and she was certain if Brian was able to track Sean down, it wasn't going to be a pleasant encounter.

"I'll go with you," Gloria said quietly.

Ruth dropped Brian and Gloria off in front of the Ocean View Resort and told Gloria that she and the others would head downtown to visit a few of the shops to stretch their legs, but would keep their cell phones close by in case they were needed.

Brian made a beeline for the front desk, the bottom of his shoes rapping loudly on the marble floor. Gloria struggled to keep up.

"Yes, I'd like to leave a message for Sean Brodwell," Brian told the clerk.

The clerk gave Brian a brief nod and then began tapping the computer keyboard in front of him. "Mr. Brodwell checked out of the hotel this morning."

Brian leaned an elbow on the counter. "Any idea where he went?"

"No sir." The desk clerk shook his head.

Brian thanked the clerk and the two of them moved to the side of the lobby. "Surely the police wouldn't let the man leave the island if Andrea is missing and he was the last person seen with her."

Brian shoved his hands in his front pants pockets and rocked back on his heels. "It could be he was taking some heat from investigators and/or Andrea's parents so he checked out."

"We need to track him down." Gloria began pacing back and forth. "But how? We need to figure out where he went."

"Or even what he looks like," Brian added.

"We could start by checking the Nantucket Morning News to see if there's an update. After that, we can check the social media sites to see if he's online."

Gloria snapped her fingers and abruptly stopped. "I've got an idea! We tail Andrea's parents. I'm sure they're still in touch with Mr. Brodwell. They'll lead us right to him."

Brian sucked in a deep breath. "It's a start. Her parents met me in this lobby. This is where they told me to go home."

"It's still early. We could hang out here, see if we can spot them either leaving the hotel or coming back." Gloria glanced around. There was a cluster of uncomfortable Victorian period furniture tucked off in the corner. "Let's wait over there."

They headed to the wingback chairs off to the side and settled in. Gloria sat so she had a bird's eye view of guests as they came and went.

The two of them sat for what seemed like forever with nary a glimpse of the Thorntons. Gloria checked her watch. "We need to take shifts," she said. "Let me see if a couple of the others can head over to give us a break and a chance to grab a quick bite to eat."

She dialed Lucy's number first.

"Did you find her or the boyfriend?" Lucy asked.

"No. Mr. Brodwell checked out of the hotel so Brian and I have been hanging out here in the hotel lobby, hoping to spot Andrea's parents so we can tail them."

"Oh, that sounds like fun," Lucy said.

"Good. I'm glad it does because Brian and I need a break. Can you and someone else take our place?"

She could hear Lucy's muffled voice in the background and then she spoke into the phone. "Margaret and I will be right there."

Ten minutes later, Margaret and Lucy arrived on scene and hurried over.

Gloria stood. "Do you remember what Andrea's parents look like?"

Lucy nodded. "Yep. Mr. Thornton is short. He has a clump of dark toupee on his head and I think he has a moustache. Mrs. Thornton is an older version of Andrea, but with a snooty demeanor." She lifted her head and peered down her nose at Gloria.

"Bingo." Gloria shifted to the side. "Remember, if they take off, you'll need to tail them but don't engage them. We're hoping they will lead us to Sean Brodwell."

"Do not engage," Margaret repeated. "We're on it."

Brian and Gloria exited the front doors and wandered down the sidewalk, in the direction of their motel, which was a short walking distance.

While they walked, Gloria attempted to calm Brian. She could see underneath his calm, cool exterior he was seething.

"We don't know the whole story," Gloria reasoned. "All we know is what David and Libby Thornton told you."

"True," Brian admitted.

Gloria pressed on. "It's not fair to Andrea. You need to give her a chance to explain herself once we find her." *If we find her,* she silently added.

Chapter 8

Gloria and Brian stumbled upon a small café on their way to the motel. Although the menu was limited, Gloria was famished and everything sounded good. She settled on a BLT with a cup of chicken noodle soup while Brian ordered a chicken bacon wrap and a side of French fries. They ordered the meal to go and carried it back to the motel.

After they finished eating, Gloria busied herself with straightening the kitchenette while Brian wandered aimlessly around the suite. She kept one eye on him and one eye on her cell phone. It was a long few hours and partway through the stakeout, Margaret and Lucy switched with Ruth and Dot.

"We'll take the next shift," Gloria told Ruth when Ruth called to confirm they were at the hotel and in position. "If not, we'll have to come up with some other plan to track down this Brodwell fellow."

Gloria thanked her friends for pitching in and was getting ready to disconnect the line when Ruth interrupted. "I've got a visual. I'll call you back."

The line disconnected.

Gloria darted into the living room where Brian was searching the internet for news stories about Andrea's disappearance. "Ruth said she spotted them."

Brian jumped out of the chair and ran to the door. "Let's roll."

His long strides left Gloria in the dust as he walked past the elevators and headed to the stairwell. By the time Gloria reached the bottom of the stairs, Brian was long gone.

She trailed after Brian, all the while praying he wouldn't approach the Thorntons a second time.

When she caught up with him inside the Ocean View Resort lobby, he was casing the joint.

Ruth and Dot were nowhere in sight.

She hurried to Brian's side. "Hopefully they were able to follow them."

Gloria pulled her cell phone from her pocket and turned it over, willing the phone to ring. "Please have something. Please."

They waited for several long, anxious moments. Gloria was getting ready to dial Ruth's cell phone when Ruth texted. "Meet me at Shady Cove Motel, 116 Davis Street. Circle 'round the rear of motel. Enter via the pool area near the back of the motel. We're hiding behind the tiki bar."

"On our way," Gloria texted her reply and then slid her cell phone in her back pocket. "Let's go!"

Gloria huffed and puffed down the sidewalk, grateful for the cool ocean breeze. "Those bicycles are sounding better and better by the minute," she gasped as she struggled to keep up with Brian and his long strides.

When they reached the Shady Cove Motel, Gloria stopped abruptly out front and studied the perimeter. "Ruth said to circle around the back and enter the pool area near the back."

"Over there." Brian pointed to a pool area to the left of the motel's front entrance. "This way." He tugged on Gloria's arm and the two power-walked down the sidewalk, making their way through the side parking lot to the rear of the motel.

There was a gate near the corner and when they got close, Gloria spotted Ruth and Dot lurking behind an empty bar area.

Ruth spotted them and motioned them over. When they reached the gate, Dot eased it open. She held a finger to her lips and pointed toward the pool. "They're over there."

The trio crept behind the tiki bar and joined Ruth, who was peeking around the side of a pole. "See them over there at the corner patio table?"

Gloria followed Ruth's gaze to the three people seated close to one another. They appeared to be having a serious conversation. "Those aren't the Thorntons."

Ruth's mouth dropped open. "You're kidding."

Gloria grinned. "I am. That's them."

Dot punched her in the arm. "Not funny."

"You're right."

"I wish we had a pair of binoculars," Gloria said.

"We do." Ruth reached into her oversize bag and handed a pair to Gloria. "I figured these might come in handy."

"I should've known." Gloria placed the binoculars to her eyes and adjusted the dial. She confirmed the Thornton's identity and then slid her gaze to the man who was with them.

He wasn't a bad looking fellow with sandy brown hair, a chiseled chin and hollow cheeks. He was tall...lanky would be a better description. His long, thin legs jutted out from under the table. Judging from the expression on his face, the trio wasn't having a pleasant conversation.

The man kept shifting his gaze, his eyes skimming the perimeter of the motel. Gloria wondered if he somehow sensed their presence, although they were hidden behind the tiki bar.

Because of his height, Brian was slightly visible. Gloria hoped the Thorntons wouldn't look over and notice him glaring at them. "I ought to walk over there, grab him by the throat and force him to tell me what he did with Andrea and then punch his lights out."

"You can't do that," Dot gasped. "You'll end up getting arrested."

"We need to follow him," Ruth said. "He may be able to lead us to Andrea."

"I agree," Gloria said.

Ruth eased to a standing position. "I need my van. I've been dying to try my new gadgets and this stakeout will be the perfect opportunity."

Dot and Ruth decided to head back to the motel to retrieve the van and update the others while Brian and Gloria stayed put to keep an eye on Sean Brodwell.

The two women snuck around the back of the motel and Brian and Gloria settled in to wait.

Gloria's phone began to beep. It was Paul. "I need to take this call in case it's about Allie." Brian nodded, never taking his eyes off his prey while Gloria tiptoed along the back of the motel where she could carry on a normal conversation and not draw attention to herself.

"Hi Paul."

"Hello Gloria. I wanted to check in and make sure you arrived in Nantucket without mishap," he said.

"We're fine." She eyed the side of the motel nervously. She couldn't see Brian and hoped he was staying put. "We still haven't found Andrea but we did find a friend of hers who is here on the island. He was with her when she went missing."

She went on to explain to Paul it was an old boyfriend and how Brian teeter-tottered between wanting to leave and wanting to punch Sean Brodwell's lights out.

"We haven't had a chance to use Ruth's spy equipment. She's on her way back to our motel to get her van since we have a visual on the Thorntons and the ex," Gloria explained. "I'm sorry. I keep rattling on. The big question is how is Allie?"

"She's fine. She's raring to get back to work but the doctor wants her to come in for a check-up before he releases her back to work," Paul said. "Allie's fine but Mally is a mess."

Gloria's heart plummeted. "What happened to Mally?"

"She chased one of the squirrels into the field between the garden and the root cellar. I guess I never noticed but there's a row of sand burs on the other side of the cellar. She plowed right into them and her fur is covered with them."

"Oh my gosh! Poor thing," Gloria said.

"Poor us. Allie and I have been picking out the burs all morning. Some of the burs were imbedded in her fur and we had to cut them out so Mally has an interesting pattern to her fur. You may want to take her to the groomer to fix up what we've done."

Gloria envisioned chunks of Mally's soft glossy fur piled up on the kitchen floor. "I will. Don't worry about it. Do what you have to do." She'd burned the sand bur weeds a year or so back after reading it was the only way to get rid of them. It was apparent she had missed a few. "You'll have to torch them to get them out."

"You want me to set Mally's fur on fire?' Paul joked.

"The burs, not Mally," Gloria said.

They discussed how Paul was going to burn that portion of the property and had moved onto the weather when Gloria caught a glimpse of Ruth and Dot out of the corner of her eye as they hurried around the side of the building. "I better get going. Ruth is back with her spy-mobile," she said. "I'll call later this evening to check on you and see how Mally and Allie are doing."

"Okay. I love you," Paul said.

"I love you, too." Gloria pressed the *end* button and slid the phone into her purse.

"How is Allie?" Dot asked and pointed to Gloria's purse.

"Allie is healing but Mally is a mess." Gloria briefly explained her pooch's latest predicament.

"We better get back to Brian. I left him to keep tabs on Sean Brodwell while I talked to Paul. I've been on the phone since you left."

Gloria led the way and they strolled toward the tiki bar. "How long were you gone?"

"About half an hour," Ruth said. "It was a long walk back to the motel and then we had to explain to the others what had happened."

They rounded the corner and Gloria stopped in the spot where she'd last seen Brian. He was gone. "He's gone."

"I hope he didn't..." Gloria was about to say *confront the suspect* but the eerie wail of police sirens interrupted her and a burning heat crept up her neck. She ran toward the pool area, her eyes scanning the perimeter. It was empty.

Ruth hurried down the sidewalk in front of the motel room doors. Dot was hot on Ruth's heels.

Gloria circled the pool area and when she rounded the last corner, a police cruiser careened into the motel parking lot and came to an abrupt halt in front of the office.

A small cluster of people had gathered in front of one of the motel rooms, near the center of the long strip.

Two officers exited the patrol car and strode to the group of people, who parted to let the officers through.

By the time Gloria reached the crowd, Ruth and Dot were already there. Gloria circled the onlookers, peering over their shoulders as she tried to see inside the motel room.

Gloria's feeling of impending doom turned to horror as she caught a glimpse of a body lying on the motel bed. The officers were standing in the doorway, talking to a third person...Brian.

Gloria eased past the gawkers as she attempted to get close enough to hear what the officers and Brian were saying. It was then she realized the person lying face up on the bed was Sean Brodwell.

Chapter 9

Things moved at breakneck speed after that. Another police car arrived, along with an ambulance.

One of the officers herded the growing crowd of bystanders off to one side to allow the emergency personnel, who were carrying a stretcher, to make their way inside the motel room.

Brian, flanked by two officers, exited the motel room and the trio made their way to the first police car on scene. One of the officers held the door while Brian slid into the back of the patrol car. After shutting the door, the officers climbed in the front.

“They’re taking him down to the police station,” Dot whispered.

"This is bad." Ruth stated the obvious.

Gloria watched until the patrol car pulled out of the motel parking lot and disappeared from sight before turning her attention to the motel room. Two more uniformed officers stood in the doorway, blocking the onlookers view of what was going on inside.

A short time later, two solemn-faced emergency personnel exited the room, carrying the stretcher. A sheet covered the stretcher and Gloria caught a glimpse of a man's hand. She shifted to the side and watched as they carefully loaded the stretcher into the back of the ambulance before making their way to the front.

The ambulance coasted out of the parking lot and onto the street. There were no lights or sirens, indicating there was no reason to hurry. Their passenger had expired.

Ruth tugged on Gloria's arm and the three of them stepped off to the side, out of earshot of the other people still lingering near what Gloria suspected was now an active crime scene. “They think Brian had something to do with the man’s death.”

“We weren’t gone long,” Dot shook her head. “Surely Brian did not kill that man. Clobber him maybe, but kill him?”

Gloria rubbed her brow. “I didn’t hear anything like a gunshot or screams.” She began to pace back and forth as she mulled over what she’d seen. “What was it? Half an hour between the time I left Brian behind the tiki bar and now?”

“That would be plenty of time to kill someone,” Ruth pointed out.

“The show is over folks. It’s time to leave the area.” One of the uniformed officers began waving his hands in an attempt to disperse the crowd.

“Let’s head to the van.” Ruth motioned them to her van, parked on the other side of the parking lot. She opened the side door and waited for Dot and Gloria to climb in before following them inside and sliding the door shut. "This is a perfect surveillance location."

Lining the sides of the van were what appeared to be television monitors.

"Check this out." Ruth dropped to her knees and crawled to the far side of the center bench seat. She pressed a lever on the side of the seat and it folded in half. She slid the seat forward and then back. It disappeared into the floor of the van.

Ruth ran her hand along the van wall, just below the bottom edge of one of the television screens. She unclasped a hook and a small bench seat flopped down. "Lower the other one." She waved to the left, to the back of the side wall.

Gloria dropped onto all fours and crawled to the back. She unhooked a latch and another bench seat flopped out.

Ruth shifted to the side. "Dot, you can sit over here."

On the other side of the van was a compact set of wall panels that contained an array of levers, switches, knobs and handles. "I feel like I'm in a gadget mobile," Dot said.

"I need to fiddle with a few more switches and we'll be good to go." Ruth mumbled under her breath as she turned her cell phone on and began tapping the screen.

The whir of machinery and flashes of light filled the interior of the van as it came to life. "I've only tried this a couple times so bear with me."

Gloria caught Dot's eye and Dot shook her head.

"Okay. I think we're in business." Ruth placed her cell phone in her lap and began twisting a dial on the front panel of one of the wall monitors. A small whirring noise filled the van and beams of light flooded the interior of the van as a round disk slowly rose from the center of the van's roof. "Bingo."

Images of the motel and parking lot filled the various screens. One showed a street view. There was a second shot of the motel entrance and a third of the motel rooms themselves.

Ruth nudged her chair to the side and settled in front of the screen that showed the open motel room door and the police officers standing on the sidewalk out front. “Good. We have a clear visual. Now we need a little sound.” She turned to Dot. “See the dial labeled ext. audio? Turn it on.”

Dot nodded and then turned the dial Ruth indicated. The interior of the van filled with street noise and cars passing by.

Ruth shook her head. “Whoops. I’ve got it on the wrong one.” She pointed to a lever to the left of the knob. “Push on the one labeled ‘RQ’ and flip up the one that says ‘FQ.’”

“Let me guess. Rear quadrant and front quadrant,” Gloria said.

Ruth winked and gave Gloria a thumbs up. “You got it.”

The street noise vanished, replaced by the sounds of voices. The officers were talking to one another. “Now nudge the dial up just a little.” Ruth pinched her thumb and index finger together.

Dot rolled her eyes but followed Ruth’s instructions. “This is too much.”

“Shh.” Ruth held a finger to her lips as the sounds of the officers’ voices echoed in the van.

“...at first it was a drug overdose but once I saw the pillow covering the victim’s face.”

Another unidentified voice continued. “Nice, clean, quiet killer.”

“Yeah. The victim looks like a clean-cut guy. So does the suspect.” The first voice answered. “Those are the ones you gotta watch out for.”

The voices faded away and the women listened for several long moments in an attempt to glean additional clues from the investigators, but Ruth's audio equipment wasn't able to capture the sounds inside the motel room.

The television monitors were crystal clear and the women watched as the investigators moved around the interior of the motel room.

Finally, the investigators and officers exited the motel room. Two of the officers headed to the motel lobby while the crime scene investigators hopped into their van and drove off.

Dot scooted across the floor of the van. "I've got to use the restroom."

"There's one near the pool area." Gloria jabbed her finger on the television screen. "It's back there, right next to the tiki bar."

"I'll be right back." Dot swung the side door open and climbed out. She hurried across the parking lot and to the sidewalk on the other side.

Gloria watched as her friend stopped abruptly in front of the motel room...the motel room where Sean Brodwell's body had been found.

Dot glanced around and then opened her purse. She pulled out her cell phone and tiptoed over to the motel room window.

"They left the curtains open," Ruth said. Sure enough, the curtains to the motel room were wide open.

Dot lifted her cell phone and pointed it at the window.

"She's taking pictures," Gloria said. "Good girl!"

Ruth and Gloria watched as Dot took a step back and lifted her camera a second time.

"Hey!" A male voice echoed through the speakers.

"Uh-oh. Busted," Ruth said.

Dot pivoted as she turned to see who was yelling.

It was the two police officers. They began jogging toward Dot.

"They must've realized they forgot to shut the curtains," Gloria said.

It was almost like watching in slow motion as Dot darted down the sidewalk and away from the police officers. She rounded the corner and disappeared from sight.

The cops were in hot pursuit.

Gloria scrambled to the door. "We need a diversion."

Ruth and Gloria stumbled out of the van and raced across the parking lot, to the side of the building.

They rounded the corner and came face-to-face with the police officers, who were pounding on the outside of the women's restroom door.

"The men's restroom is over here," Ruth said.

One of the cops stopped pounding long enough to shoot Ruth a dirty glare before he began pounding again.

Gloria's head spun as she tried to find a way to help Dot. "I'm going to report you," she threatened. The cops ignored her.

"We can wait here all day," the cop yelled at the locked door.

Moments later, a calm, cool, collected Dot emerged from the restroom. "What is all the ruckus out here?"

"Give me your phone." One of the officers, the taller of the two, held out his hand.

"No." Dot shook her head.

"I'll take you down to the precinct and charge you with tampering with police evidence." The officer turned to his partner. "Go shut those curtains before some other Nosy Nelly decides to start snooping around."

The second officer nodded and disappeared around the corner.

Dot opened her purse, reached inside and pulled out her cell phone. She dropped it in the cop's hand.

"Show me the pictures you took."

"This is ridiculous," Dot said. Not wanting to push her luck and end up joining Brian down at the precinct, she switched her cell phone on, tapped the screen and then handed it to the officer.

He gazed at the small screen and handed it back. "Show me how to erase it."

Dot let out an exaggerated breath as she took the phone from the man and fiddled with the screen. "It's gone."

"*All* of them," the officer answered.

"Fine." Dot fumbled with the screen and then finally looked up. "They're all gone. Here, you can check by scrolling the screen."

Gloria sucked in a breath as she watched the officer do exactly that. He handed the phone back. "I'm going to let you off with a warning. If I see you snooping around here again, I'll haul you off to jail and charge you with tampering with a police investigation." He turned on his heel and marched down the sidewalk.

Dot stuck her tongue out at his retreating back. "Spoil sport."

Ruth followed him to the end of the building and gazed around the corner. "He's gone." She hurried to Dot's side. "Did you get a chance to look at the pictures?"

"Nope." Dot shook her head. "I did something even better..." She grinned wickedly. "While I was in the bathroom, I forwarded copies to Gloria's cell phone."

Gloria smiled. "A girl after my own heart." She patted Dot on the arm. "I see all my years of training have finally paid off."

The women wandered back to the van, passing by the officers who were climbing into the patrol car.

Dot gave a jaunty wave. "Now all we'll have to do is spring Brian and expand our investigation into Andrea's disappearance and Sean Brodwell's murder."

The trio climbed into Ruth's van and drove back to their motel where they met up with the rest of the girls to discuss what had transpired and to come up with some sort of plan to not only spring Brian, but also find Andrea and uncover Sean's killer.

Gloria remembered how the officers had mentioned drugs in the motel room. Brian was not a drug user or a drug peddler. If what the officers said was true, she had a sneaky suspicion Sean Brodwell's death had something to do with the drugs.

Their first priority was to figure out where the officers had taken Brian and then resume their search for Andrea. The longer Andrea was missing, the more concerned Gloria became.

"I'm going to call Paul to see how long the authorities can detain Brian and on what grounds." She dialed Paul's cell phone number and he answered right away. "I was getting ready to call you."

He went on. "You're never going to believe who just showed up on our porch steps."

"Who?"

"Andrea," he said. "She's sitting at our kitchen table."

Chapter 10

Gloria nearly dropped the phone. "You're kidding."

"Nope. Hang on. I'll put her on."

There was a moment of silence before a hesitant Andrea came on the line. "Hello?"

Gloria said the first thing that popped into her head. "I can't believe you're in Belhaven."

"I couldn't take it anymore. My parents were driving me crazy, pressuring me to move back to New York. The last straw was when they surprised me with my ex-boyfriend, Sean."

"Sean Brodwell," Gloria said.

"What a jerk," Andrea groaned. "Hopefully he doesn't follow me to Belhaven."

"I don't think that will be a problem," Gloria said.

"I'm calling my parents to let them know I'm home," Andrea said. "I know they're worried but I can't believe they filed a missing person's report. I told them if they kept it up, I was gonna leave."

"Well, they did and I'm sure they're very concerned," Gloria said. "I'm glad you're home and safe. Now stay put until we get back there. We've tried calling you for days now. Why didn't you answer your cell phone?"

"I forgot my phone charger. I was in such a hurry, I forgot and left it in the hotel room," Andrea said. "Paul has already given me the fatherly lecture about scaring people half to death and being a responsible adult."

"How do you think Brian will react?" Andrea fretted. "I didn't know you were going to drive to Nantucket."

"We wanted to surprise you, to talk some sense into you," Gloria said.

"Is Brian there?" Andrea asked.

Gloria glanced at the others, who were staring intently at her. "Brian is not here. We have another slight problem. I'm glad you're safe dear. We'll talk later. Could you put Paul back on?"

"Sure." There was a moment of silence. "I'm sorry Gloria," Andrea apologized.

"It's all right dear. We're glad you're safe," Gloria repeated.

Paul's deep voice echoed through the line. "When are you heading back home?"

"I'm not sure. Can we talk privately?"

Dot hopped off the sofa and Gloria shook her head. "Not you," she mouthed as she pointed at the phone.

"Of course." Gloria could hear Paul on the move. "Go ahead. I'm on the porch. Andrea is inside chatting with Allie."

"Andrea's ex was found murdered inside his motel room," Gloria said. "The police took Brian to the police station for questioning."

"Brian was involved?" Paul asked.

"He's the one who found the man's body," Gloria said.

Paul let out a low whistle. "Huh," was all he managed to say.

"We haven't talked to him yet," Gloria said. "I wondered what grounds the police could hold him on."

"What happened?"

"I wish I knew," Gloria sighed. "By the time we got to the scene, the police were already there and Brian was standing in the doorway of the deceased's motel room."

They talked for several more moments and Gloria told him they were going to drive down to the police station to try to help.

"Don't do anything to get yourself arrested," Paul warned.

Gloria shuddered. "That's the last thing I want to happen."

After she disconnected the line, Gloria faced her friends. "Andrea showed up on our doorstep. She said her mother and father were pressuring her to move back to New York and wouldn't let up. The last straw was when they 'surprised' her with the arrival of her now deceased ex-boyfriend."

"Does she know he's dead?" Rose asked.

"I think Paul will tell her and then have her call her parents to assure them she is safe," Gloria said. "Poor Paul, caught right in the middle."

"Again," Lucy said.

"As usual," Margaret quipped.

"What about Brian?" Alice asked.

"We need to drive to the police station," Gloria said. She turned to Dot. "You need to stay put. I'm afraid if you show up, the officer who took your cell phone will follow through with his threat and arrest you."

Dot nodded fearfully. "I'll hang out here and hold down the fort."

Rose patted Dot's hand. "I'll stay with you."

"We can't all go," Lucy said.

"Ruth has to drive. Alice should go," Gloria said.

"Yes, Brian." Alice stood. "He need me. I will go."

The group decided Lucy, Ruth, Alice and Gloria would head to the police station to try to spring Brian.

After a quick internet search for police stations on the small island, Ruth jotted down the address to enter into the GPS and the four of them headed out. They made it to the van when Lucy abruptly stopped. "Wait a minute. I better leave my gun here."

She hurried across the parking lot and disappeared inside her motel room.

"Did she say she was going to leave her gun behind?" Gloria asked.

Ruth stuck a hand on her hip. "And you thought I was bad."

Lucy returned moments later and Gloria climbed into the passenger seat while Alice and Lucy got into the back.

"Why in the world did you bring a gun?" Gloria flipped the visor down and peered at her friend in the mirror.

"Protection," Lucy patiently explained. "There are a lot of crazies these days. It's only one little gun."

Alice made the symbol of a cross across her chest. "Dear Lord, please help us."

"Only one little gun," Gloria said. "A gun is a gun. Big, little, sawed off, semi-automatic."

Lucy held up a hand. "Okay. Maybe it was a mistake, but it's too late now."

They rode the distance to the station in silence.

Gloria prayed they would find Brian at the station and that the police would release him after questioning. She had checked her cell phone several times to make sure she hadn't missed his call and suspected the police were still grilling him.

They pulled into the visitor parking lot and Gloria studied the patrol cars parked off to the side. The markings on the patrol cars were the same ones she'd observed at Brodwell's motel.

"I'll wait here," Ruth said as she shifted the van into park. The other three exited the van and headed up the steps and through the front door of the police station.

Gloria held the door for Alice and Lucy. The smell of fresh floor varnish assaulted Gloria's nose and she waved her hand in front of her face. "Yuck."

She trailed behind Alice and Lucy as they approached the counter. A uniformed officer looked up. "May I help you?"

"Yes, uh, our friend was brought to the station for questioning and we wondered when he might be released," Gloria said.

The man peered at the trio of women over the rim of his glasses. "What is the name?"

"Brian Sellers," Lucy said.

The man nodded and then tapped on the keyboard as he gazed at the computer screen. "Yes. Mr. Sellers is here. He's with Detective Flint. Let me check on him."

He disappeared through a swinging door and Gloria headed to the corkboard on the far wall. She studied the missing persons' flyers and noted Andrea's photo at the very top.

"Should I tell them Andrea has been found?" Gloria spun back around.

"I wouldn't," Lucy said. "Her parents filed the missing person's report. Let them handle it."

"You're probably right." Gloria shifted to the side and stared at the Most Wanted postings. There was only a handful. "They must not have a lot of crime on the island."

"Mr. Sellers will be free to leave shortly if you'd like to wait." The officer returned and pointed to a row of chairs under the bulletin board.

Gloria slumped into a chair and then fumbled inside her purse in search of her cell phone. She pulled the phone out, tapped the screen and studied the messages Dot had sent her, the ones with the pictures of the inside of the motel room.

Alice paced while Lucy took Gloria's place and studied the posters on the wall. "Check this guy out."

Gloria lifted her head. "Huh?"

Lucy pointed at one of the posters. "Based on your description, this guy looks a lot like Andrea's ex."

Chapter 11

Gloria hopped out of the chair and peered over Lucy's shoulder. "Nah. Not even close." She pointed at the forehead. "His face is too round. Brodwell's face was long and thin."

"I guess you would know since I didn't get an actual visual on him."

"Ah, there he is," Alice said.

Brian, accompanied by a uniformed officer, stepped into the lobby. Both men wore solemn expressions. The officer turned to face Brian. "We may need to ask you a few more questions so you'll need to stick around."

"Of course." Brian nodded and then turned to Alice, Gloria and Lucy. "I'm ready."

The four of them exited through the front door and down the small set of steps.

Ruth gave a small wave as they made their way to the vehicle.

Brian opened the passenger side door and slid into the seat. "Talk about being in the wrong place at the wrong time."

"What happened?" Alice asked as she reached for her seatbelt.

"I'd rather tell this story once so I'll wait until we get back to the motel."

"I don't blame you." Gloria switched her phone back on, slipped her reading glasses on and studied the pictures of Brodwell's motel room. She could make out an unmade bed. The top of the dresser, in front of the bed was cluttered. She tapped the screen to enlarge the picture but the glare from the motel room window obscured part of the picture.

She swiped the screen to view the second picture. The second one was even blurrier, probably because by that time, the police had spotted Dot and she was on the run.

Gloria smiled as she remembered Dot running from the cops. "I wish we could replay the moment when Dot was taking a picture of the inside of the motel room and the police officers hollered at her," she said.

Ruth glanced in the rearview mirror. "We can. I recorded it."

"Why am I not surprised?" Gloria asked.

The Craggy Manor parking lot was crowded and Ruth drove around the building twice before she found a spot she deemed "safe" for her beloved van. On one side was a curb and on the other, a high-end sports car. She surveyed her surroundings before shutting the engine off. "This spot looks as good as any."

"I still don't get it. If this thing is bullet proof, it should be ding proof," Gloria said as she grabbed the side door handle.

"I'm not taking any chances." Ruth dropped her sunglasses in the center console and turned to Brian. "Be careful when you open the door."

Brian slid out of the passenger seat and made his way to the front of the vehicle. “You have a bubble on the top. I never noticed it before.”

Gloria joined him. “It’s new. It’s a spy camera that pops up and has a 360-degree view of the surroundings.”

“And the van is bullet proof but Ruth won’t test it,” Alice said.

Ruth clicked the key fob and locked the van before leading the way. “I agreed to test the features. It was part of the deal, but I can’t bring myself to do it…not yet.”

The door to Dot, Ruth and Rose’s suite was open and Gloria could hear the murmur of voices. She pushed the door open and stepped inside.

Dot and Margaret were sitting at the small table. Rose hovered near a small hotplate located on the kitchenette counter.

"You sprung him." Dot hopped out of her chair and hugged Brian. "Thank goodness they didn't throw you in jail."

"They couldn't charge me with anything," Brian said. "Lack of evidence." He ran a hand through his hair. "Believe me, they wanted to."

"Have a seat." Margaret stood and offered Brian her chair.

"No thanks. I've been sitting for hours. It feels good to stretch my legs."

"What happened?" Gloria asked. "Start at the beginning, when I left you near the tiki bar so I could talk to Paul."

Brian leaned against the wall and crossed his arms. "Well, right after you walked away, David and Libby Thornton left. Brodwell was alone. He appeared agitated and my gut told me something was going to happen so I hung back. He began to pace as he looked around. It was as if he sensed my presence."

"He exited the pool area and stepped into the parking lot. I trailed behind but waited near the corner of the building until I saw him unlock one of the motel room doors. From where I was standing, I couldn't tell which one he went into. He turned back and stared directly down the sidewalk. I could've sworn he spotted me so I ducked back behind the wall and waited."

Lucy interrupted. "Did the Thorntons spot you?"

"Nope." Brian shook his head. "They had already climbed into a dark sedan and drove off."

"Go on," Alice prompted.

"I hung around and then made my way to the back of the building to check on Gloria. She was still talking on the phone with her back to me so I walked toward the front again."

"I waited another five, ten minutes and kept thinking Gloria, Ruth and Dot would show up but you never did so I started down the sidewalk. When I got halfway down, I noticed one of the motel room doors was ajar so I nudged it open with my foot. That's when I found him."

"Brodwell," Gloria said.

"Yep. He was on the bed, sprawled out on his back, but at an odd angle. I didn't touch anything and didn't step inside. I called his name and when he didn't respond, I dialed 911."

"So between the time you spotted him entering his motel room, looking nervous and glancing over his shoulder and the time you walked down the sidewalk, someone murdered him."

"Bingo," Brian nodded. "From what the investigator said, it appears he suffocated. I have racked my brain trying to remember if I saw anyone lurking about or looking suspicious but there was nothing."

"Unless whoever killed Brodwell was waiting inside the motel room," Margaret said.

"Yep."

Brian walked over to the window and peered out. "I wonder if the same person who murdered Brodwell kidnapped Andrea or worse."

Gloria and Alice's eyes met. "We have some good news," Gloria said.

"Andrea is in Belhaven," Alice blurted out. "She is home."

Brian spun around, his eyes wide with disbelief. "You're kidding," he sputtered.

"No. Her parents were pressuring her to move back to New York and when they sprung the ex-boyfriend on her, she decided enough was enough so she plotted her escape," Gloria said. "She had no idea we were on our way here and planned to call her parents once she was back home."

"We just missed her," Alice said.

"Why didn't she answer our calls or texts to at least let us know she was safe?" Brian asked.

"She was in such a hurry to escape the island, she forgot her cell phone charger in the hotel room," Gloria explained. "She wasn't able to charge it until she arrived home."

"So we can go home now." Rose, who had been rummaging around in the cupboards of the small kitchenette, reached inside and pulled out a glass plate.

"No can do." Brian shook his head. "I can't leave until the police clear me as a suspect since I found the body."

"Wait until they find out the dead man was your fiancée's ex-boyfriend," Dot said.

"It doesn't look good," Lucy agreed.

"We need to figure out who killed Brodwell," Gloria said.

"And why," Ruth reached into her backpack, sitting on the floor next to her, unzipped the top and pulled out her laptop. "As Gloria likes to say motive and opportunity, but first we need to find out a little more about Sean Brodwell."

"Andrea would know him," Gloria said. She turned to Brian. "I'm sure Paul or her parents have told her Brodwell was found dead in his motel room. You should give her a call."

"What if she thinks I killed him?" Brian asked.

"You know she won't believe that for a second, Brian." Alice patted his arm. "She was on her way home...to you."

"True." Brian glanced uneasily around the room. "I suppose I could give her a call."

"You don't want all of us listening in," Gloria said. "Why don't you head back to our room so you can have some privacy?"

"I want to listen in," Ruth argued.

The others shot her a dark stare. "All right."

Brian exited the suite and closed the door behind him.

Chapter 12

Gloria waited until the door was shut. "We should pray about this." She waved the group to gather near the kitchen area. They joined hands and bowed their heads. "Dear Heavenly Father, we pray for Brian and Andrea, Lord. We pray you heal the hurt feelings, the wounds and open the lines of communication. We pray for forgiveness on both sides and thank you, in advance, for answered prayers."

"We also pray you quickly clear Brian's name in the murder investigation," Dot added.

"Amen," Lucy finished.

Gloria released her hold on Rose and Lucy's hands and stared uneasily at the door. "We need to take a look at the pictures Dot was able to snap of the inside of Brodwell's motel room."

Ruth, who had eased back into the chair and sat facing her laptop, looked up. "Shoot them to me in an email and I'll open them up so we can view them on my laptop screen."

"Good idea." Gloria reached for her cell phone and the overpowering stench of burnt fish mingled with garlic blasted her in the face. She began to gag. "Oh my gosh! What is that disgusting smell?"

"This?" Rose picked up a burning candle and waved it in the air.

Lucy, who was standing closest to Rose, stumbled backward. "Ugh." She pinched the sides of her nose and gasped for air.

"What a horrid odor!" Margaret scrambled out of her chair and bolted toward the door. She flung the door open, stumbled onto the sidewalk and gulped the fresh air.

"It's my own special candle," Rose said as she calmly set the candle on top of the hot plate. "It's fermented herring, a layer of minced garlic and a layer of anise."

Dot ran out of the room and followed Margaret onto the sidewalk.

"I use it to ward off bad spirits." Rose studied the ceiling. "I'm sensing a bad presence. I'm not sure if it's emanating from this room or the entire motel."

"It could ward off bad spirits and vampires," Lucy joked, still pinching her nostrils shut.

"Maybe vampires." Rose's eyes slid to Alice, who caught the sly look.

"You think I'm a vampire?" Alice gasped as she jabbed her chest.

Gloria stepped between the women. "I'm sure she didn't mean you," she said. "Please put that out before one of us loses our lunch."

"Okay." Rose reluctantly blew out the candle. "But if something bad happens, don't blame me."

"Something bad?" Ruth shook her head. "What else could possibly happen that hasn't already?"

"Let's adjourn to the other suite to give this place a chance to air out." Gloria waved her hand in front of her face.

The women headed to the suite next door. Ruth grabbed her laptop off the table, bringing up the rear. "I got the pictures." She placed her open laptop on the table.

"I don't see any blood or guts," Lucy said as she peered over Ruth's shoulder. She pointed to the dresser. "Did you notice all of those pill bottles?"

"We heard the cops say something about drugs," Gloria said. "They said something about an overdose and then mentioned another piece of evidence but I couldn't figure out what they were talking about."

"Maybe Brodwell discovered Andrea had returned home and became despondent," Alice theorized.

"But Brian said his body was lying at an odd angle," Dot said.

"Hello?" Brian stepped into the motel room. "You moved."

"Yeah. Rose is warding off evil spirits in their suite so we had to vacate," Gloria said. "How did the conversation with Andrea go?"

"Okay, I guess," Brian said. "We agreed that once I return home, we're going to have a nice, long heart-to-heart talk."

"What did she say about Brodwell's death? Did she know?"

"Yes. Her parents told her when she called to tell them she was safe and in Belhaven."

"And?" Gloria prompted.

"They told her they think I killed him," Brian said.

"Whew!" Lucy blew air through thinned lips. "That's terrible."

Brian went on to explain Andrea told him Sean Brodwell was acting odd during their brief time together, before she managed to escape. He kept commenting to her that he was considering moving out of New York and into the country, away from the hustle and bustle.

"She thought it was unusual since he was a city boy through and through. She also said he seemed very nervous and he was constantly looking over his shoulder."

"Which is the same comment you made," Gloria pointed out.

"I think he was a drug dealer," Margaret said. "Could be he owed someone a bunch of money."

"We need his address or at least the area where he lived so we can dig into his past," Ruth said.

"Come over here and look at the pictures Dot was able to snap of the inside of Brodwell's motel room." Gloria motioned to Brian.

The girls shifted to the side and Brian leaned over Ruth's shoulder as he studied the pictures. Two of them were semi-clean shots and the third was mostly a blur.

"Where did you get these?" Brian asked as he studied the pictures.

"The investigators forgot to shut the drapes to Brodwell's motel room so Dot snapped a couple pictures of the inside before the police started chasing her." Gloria chuckled. "Ruth has the footage. Later tonight, we'll pop some popcorn and settle in for a replay of the action."

Dot popped Gloria on the arm. "Don't you dare."

"It looks the same, minus the body." Brian tapped his finger on the screen. "I don't recall seeing that."

Gloria leaned in to see where he was pointing. It was a square sheet of plastic, sitting right next to one of the bed pillows. "Plastic...pillow. You don't recall hearing any noises, like someone screaming, or gunshots so his death was quick and quiet."

"Brodwell headed to his room. He kept looking around, thinking someone was following him." Gloria straightened her back and tapped the side of her chin thoughtfully. "What if he wasn't being followed but instead, someone was waiting for him inside his motel room?"

Lucy picked up. "He locked himself in his room. Maybe he was nervous so he popped a pill and crawled onto his bed."

"The person lurking inside caught him off guard, placed the plastic over his face and suffocated him," Ruth finished. "He was already drugged up. It wouldn't take much to finish the deed."

"How did the killer get into his room?" Gloria asked. "I'm sure Brodwell didn't leave the door unlocked."

"Hang on a second." Lucy eased past Gloria and studied the screen. "The motel room door is open, but you can see they use the key cards."

Gloria nodded. "Yep." She knew right where Lucy was going with her line of thinking. "Someone picked the lock and let themselves in."

"Bingo." Lucy grabbed one of the room cards from the table and headed to the door. "Allow me to demonstrate."

The others followed Lucy out of the motel room and crowded around her on the sidewalk.

Lucy pulled the door shut. "Our rooms are also key card access." She pointed at the door. "Note the door is locked."

"Correct," Ruth said.

Lucy grasped the door handle and pressed down. She slipped the room card into the doorjamb and began wiggling it as she pressed lightly. Moments later, the door popped open. "Easy peasy."

Alice's jaw dropped. "That is scary."

The group headed back inside and Gloria closed the door behind them. She flipped the deadbolt. "Opportunity equals anyone. Motive equals drugs. Now we have to find more out about Sean Brodwell."

Chapter 13

Ruth settled in front of the computer once again. She exited out of the photos after saving them to a file she named *Drug Dealer Death.* She rubbed her hands together and her fingers hovered over the keyboard. "Where do we start?"

"Social media," Gloria suggested.

"Good answer." Ruth's fingers flew over the keyboard as she searched Sean Brodwell's social profile. His last post had been the previous day where he begged his family and friends to help him find his missing "lost love."

"Unbelievable," Brian gritted out.

"Remember, Andrea snuck away from him," Gloria said. "He was disillusioned."

There were several posted photos. Some were of him alone, looking smug. In several others, he was posing with smiling females, his arm draped around their shoulders.

Ruth scrolled slowly through the screen while they studied the posts.

"Wait!" Margaret said. "Back up."

Ruth scrolled up and read the caption under a picture of a smiling Brodwell. "It says 'Headed to NT for a little R&R, mixed with a little business.'"

"I wonder what kind of business," Gloria murmured.

Ruth scrolled through several more posts and then they dropped off, right around the beginning of the year. She hovered over the "x" to click out of the screen when Gloria stopped her. "Wait a minute. Go back to the R&R post. I want to see who liked it."

"Good idea." Lucy snapped her fingers.

There were several likes and Ruth systematically made her way down the list as she clicked on each person's name. None of them jumped out as particularly suspect. "It looks like a dead end."

"Except for the comment about mixing business with pleasure," Alice said. "I remember him now. He and Andrea dated for a short time. Her parents, they love Sean. His family come from big money in the Hamptons, but Andrea, she think he too..." She paused, searching for the right word.

"Snobbish?" Gloria prompted.

"Yes and phony, like he not real." Alice nodded.

"We need to track Brodwell's steps from the moment he stepped foot on the island, maybe even try to get our hands on a list of the passengers who boarded the shuttle the day he arrived," Gloria said.

"The best person to ask would be Andrea." She grabbed her cell phone off the table and texted her young friend, asking her what she could remember of her brief time with Brodwell. "I'm sure police will want to question Andrea, as well."

"You're right, given the fact she vanished without telling anyone and the last person she had contact with on the island is now dead," Brian grimaced.

"Will the police force her to return to Nantucket?" Ruth wondered aloud.

"They can't force her," Brian answered. "But it would make her look a lot less guilty if she agreed to answer some questions."

Gloria's cell phone chirped. She picked it up, slipped her reading glasses on and studied the screen. "According to Andrea, she wasn't aware Brodwell was on the island until a few days ago when her parents surprised her during dinner and he showed up."

"He could have been here longer, though." She slowly scrolled through Andrea's lengthy text. "She said she was so shocked when he asked her to accompany him to the farmer's market the following morning, she didn't say no, but after returning to her room, she hatched a plan to ditch him and return home. She figured by the time her parents figured it out, she would be back in Belhaven."

"It took her a couple days on the mainland to find a one way flight back to Grand Rapids. She had no idea her parents filed a missing person's report since she'd threatened to leave if they kept pressuring her to sell her home and move back to New York." Gloria lowered the phone and gazed at Brian. "And she apologized again."

"Sounds legit," Margaret shrugged. "Her parents sound like a trip."

"They are," Alice, Gloria and Brian answered in unison.

"They won't be any help," Brian added.

Gloria's phone chirped again. "Oh, here's what Andrea knows."

Ruth reached for a pen. "I'll take notes."

"Sean checked into the Ocean View Resort and met them for dinner. During dinner, he mentioned meeting a business partner briefly after dinner and possibly the following day but assured her that the rest of the time he would be free."

"Free to what? Free to woo my girl?" Brian asked.

"We've been over this before, Brian. Andrea had nothing to do with it. She's telling us what he told her," Gloria replied before turning her attention to the phone. "She says he mentioned someone by the name of Luke and a place called Fathom, somewhere over by the marina."

There was another chirp and Gloria continued to scroll. "That's it. She said if he commented on anything else, she wasn't paying attention and was already plotting her getaway." Gloria grinned.

She set the phone down and it chirped one last time. Gloria picked it up. "One more thing. Her father is golfing buddies with the chief of police so don't expect any help from them."

Ruth's fingers were already flying over the computer keyboard. "There's no place on the island called Fathom. She said it was near the marina?"

"Yes."

"I see a couple restaurants on the marina. Barnacle Bill's Seafood Restaurant and Tides. There's nothing listed by the name of Fathom," Ruth said.

"Let's check Brodwell's profile to see if there's anyone on there named Luke." Ruth switched screens and pulled up Brodwell's profile a second time. "Blocked access. We can't see his friend's list."

"Shoot," Rose said. "I thought we wuz getting somewhere." She patted her stomach. "I'm near starvin'. I say we kill two birds with one stone...eat dinner and maybe even dig up some clues."

"I spotted some bikes in front of the motel office," Lucy headed to the door. "The marina isn't far. I don't mind renting a bike and riding."

"Me either," Gloria said.

"I'm in," Brian nodded. "A little fresh air will help clear my head."

They agreed to try Barnacle Bill's Seafood Restaurant after discovering the other restaurant, Tides, was a small seafood shack with no indoor dining.

The others headed to Ruth's van while Brian, Lucy and Gloria walked to the office. A short time later, they were coasting down the hill, toward the marina. The weather was picture perfect...perfect for an early evening bike ride.

Gloria attempted to enjoy the scenery during the ride but because it had been decades since she'd ridden a bike, she had to focus on the task at hand.

Lucy was an old pro and beat both Brian and her to the restaurant where Ruth and the others were already waiting.

Gloria slowed the bike and stopped near the edge of the parking lot and a bike rack. She slid off the bike and then pulled it into the rack. Lucy parked beside her. "The bike ride was fun," she said. "I wouldn't mind exploring the island if we have time."

The sun danced off the deep blue waters and Gloria admired the large yachts and fishing boats that filled the marina as she made her way to the entrance.

It reminded her of the recent cruise the girls had taken on board Siren of the Seas where Gloria's cousin, Millie Sanders, was assistant cruise director. It had been a wonderful vacation and the girls had discussed doing it again the following year.

She squeezed in behind Alice and waited while the hostess gathered a stack of menus and wrapped silverware, and then led them to a large table near the window that overlooked the water.

"Perfect." Gloria took an end seat and the others settled in around her. The smell of fresh seafood reminded her of Rose's candle concoction and she wrinkled her nose. "I smell Rose's candle," she joked and the others laughed.

Alice frowned. Gloria reached out and patted her hand. "Rose's candle has nothing to do with you."

"Hmpf." Alice reached for her menu and shot Rose a dark look.

Gloria opened the menu and studied the offerings. Her eyes slid past the appetizers and salads. The clambake sounded perfect...buttered lobster, sweet corn, carrots, potatoes and littleneck clams, something she'd never tried before.

She handed the server the menu after the woman jotted her order on the order pad and shifted in her chair so she had an unobstructed view of the marina. “We should ask around to see if anyone has ever heard of ‘fathom.’”

“Great idea.” Dot reached for her glass of water and rubbed her hand over the white linen tablecloth. “Do you think I should add tablecloths for dinner service?”

“In Belhaven?” Rose propped an elbow on the table. “It sounds like a lot more laundry and work to me.”

“True,” Dot said. “It was just a thought. We could hire a linen company to supply the tablecloths and then add a candle centerpiece to the tables to give it a little more ambiance during the evening dinner hours.”

“And raise your prices,” Gloria said as she reached for her glass of ice water.

Dot hadn’t raised prices at the restaurant in years. The last time Ray and she had bumped up the prices, Dot told Gloria she thought customers were going to picket in front of the restaurant.

Gloria had been hinting on and off it wasn't fair to Dot and Ray that food prices had increased but Dot didn't want to rock the boat and so far hadn't budged on her decision.

Even Rose was telling her they needed to bump up their prices. Seventy-five cents for a bottomless cup of coffee was too cheap.

Dot smoothed the napkin in her lap. "You know my thoughts on the subject," she mumbled.

The group discussed Brodwell's demise and their theories on who had murdered him. When their food arrived, the conversation ceased and Gloria shifted her plate as she studied her clambake. It looked intriguing and she was dying to dig in. The only thing that put her off was the sight of the clamshells.

Gloria tried one of the clams and then decided they weren't to her liking. Rose gladly offered to take them off her hands so Gloria scooped them onto her bread plate and passed them to her.

The lobster, potatoes, carrots and sweet corn were delectable and Gloria savored every single bite before she cleaned her plate. She finished it off with a buttery cheddar biscuit.

Brian had ordered a piece of swordfish and shared a bite with Gloria, who deemed it as delicious as her own dish.

After the server cleared the table, Gloria opted for a cup of coffee while a few of the others ordered the restaurant's specialty dessert, blueberry cobbler.

The server, a bubbly brown-haired girl, filled Gloria's coffee cup. She waited until the girl finished pouring. "You don't happen to know of a place near the marina named *Fathom*.

"Nope." She shook her pony-tailed head. "Never heard of it and I've lived here all my life." She rounded the table to add coffee to Rose's cup. "Wait! I have heard the name *Fathom*. It's not a place. It's a yacht that sails into our harbor once a week."

The lightbulb clicked on in Gloria's head. Marina...fathom. "You wouldn't happen to know who owns the yacht. Is it a local?"

"Nope. The guy comes in all alone and by boat once a week, every Wednesday, for our all you-can-eat shrimp and all-you-can drink specialty beer."

She shifted the coffee pot to her other hand. The others leaned in, hanging on every word. "He always pays in cash. Big tipper, though. He orders the same thing...an order each of the sautéed shrimp, the fried shrimp and the wood grilled shrimp. He also orders our specialty draft beer, *Billy's Bodacious Brew*. The owner, Billy Harding, worked for years perfecting the recipe and it's our best-selling brew."

The hostess began waving frantically at their server. "I better get back to work." She turned to go and then turned back. "I think Mr. Harding knows this guy, though. He always calls him *Smooth Hand Luke.*"

Chapter 14

Lucy waited until the server reached the other side of the restaurant. She leaned forward. "We're coming back tomorrow for the all-you-can-eat shrimp and to get a glimpse of this Luke fella."

"Absolutely." Gloria nodded.

Margaret dabbed at the corner of her mouth with her napkin and set it on the table next to her silverware. "I might have to try one of those bodacious brews, strictly for research purposes, of course."

Brian tossed his napkin on the table. "I'll be right back." He slid his chair out and strode across the room to the cash register.

"I wonder what he's doing," Rose said.

Gloria watched as he approached the cash register, pulled out his wallet and handed their server a card.

"I hope he's not paying for all of our meals," Margaret said as the woman swiped the card and handed it back to him.

Brian returned moments later, receipt in hand.

"You didn't buy our meals," Gloria scolded.

"I did. It's my way of saying thank you all for accompanying me. I have a feeling this posse is going to be the one to solve the mystery of Brodwell's murder so I can head home to my beautiful bride-to-be."

Gloria smiled at Brian as they walked out the door, a spring in her step. Things were starting to look up. Andrea was safe, they had some solid leads in the murder investigation and Brian wasn't in the slammer...yet.

They exited the restaurant and Gloria gazed toward the marina. "Let's take a walk on the dock." The group wandered down the sidewalk and to the end of the boat dock. Gloria was amazed at the amount of fishing gear on some of the fishing boats. She knew that Paul, who loved to fish, would have loved to bend a fisherman's ear or two for a little expert fishing advice.

She made a mental note to give her husband a call when she returned to the motel. She hoped both Allie and Mally's crises were almost over and even wondered if perhaps Andrea had thought of something else, some other piece of useful information while talking to Paul, something she may have overlooked in her texts.

The sun had set by the time Brian, Lucy and Gloria climbed onto their bikes and leisurely pedaled back to the motel. They had the entire day tomorrow to check out the island before returning to Barnacle Bill's Seafood Restaurant the following evening.

Fearing someone might steal the rented bikes, the trio eased them into Brian and Gloria's suite and parked them near the front window. They headed to the suite next door where the girls were waiting.

Margaret was sprawled out on the bed. She lifted her head. "I don't know how you had enough energy to ride that contraption back to the motel."

"The salty sea air is good for you," Lucy laughed. "You should try it."

Gloria eased into the chair in front of the table. "Margaret, you're in charge of travel and entertainment. Find something fun for us to do tomorrow."

Margaret sprung from the bed. "I thought you'd never ask. I already have several ideas." She rattled off an array of activities that made Gloria's head spin.

Several in the group wanted a less taxing day and opted to explore the local whaling museum, followed by some shopping and then lunch while Gloria, Brian, Lucy and Alice decided a bike tour, followed by a beach picnic so they could explore the beautiful island was in order.

"Alice, you are like family to the Thorntons," Dot said. "What if you stopped by the hotel tomorrow morning and tried to talk to them?"

"Great idea," Gloria said.

"I would be happy to." Alice stiffened her back. "They are good people, just very…uh…protective of Andrea."

They agreed to bike to the Ocean View Resort first thing in the morning where Alice would "surprise" them with a visit.

Gloria finally stood, lifted her hands over her head and stretched. "I'm ready to hit the hay. It has been a long day and I'm whupped."

Brian followed Gloria out of the suite and to their room. "I'm going hang around out here and give Paul a quick call. I'll meet you inside."

Brian nodded. "I want to talk to Andrea for a moment, too." He slid his key card in the door, turned the knob and stepped inside, closing the door behind him.

Gloria offered a quick prayer for another healing conversation before she pulled her phone from her purse and dialed Paul's cell phone.

It went to voice mail so she left a brief message and then wandered to the courtyard to give Brian some privacy.

A manicured path led to a spacious pool area and she started to head toward it when she remembered there was a killer on the loose so she stayed put. At least if she stayed close to the room, Brian would hear her scream if she was attacked.

Gloria shivered and reminded herself Sean Brodwell was most likely targeted and his death the result of a drug deal gone bad. Still, until the authorities apprehended the killer, no one was safe.

Her eyes scanned the parking lot and she spotted Ruth's shiny van off to one side. An overhead street light shone down on the top and she caught a glimpse of the camera bubble on top.

Gloria's phone vibrated and chirped causing her to jump. It was Paul. "How is Allie?"

"She's bound and determined to head back to work tomorrow morning, despite my objections," Paul said. "We managed to give Mally a bath and remove the rest of the burs from her fur."

"I just got back from checking on Andrea," Paul rattled off. "I'm holding down the fort but I miss you."

"I miss you, too," Gloria said with a catch in her throat as she thought of how far away her husband was. "The sooner the police clear Brian, the sooner we can get off this island and head home." She told him about their conversation with the server and how they'd uncovered a clue to the identity of the person Brodwell planned to meet while on the island.

"Maybe you should steer clear of this investigation," Paul warned. "You're in unfamiliar territory and there's a killer on the loose."

"The only thing we plan to do is head back to the restaurant, Barnacle Bill's, for dinner tomorrow to see if we can track down this Smooth Hand Luke character."

"So you're moving full steam ahead with an investigation," Paul said.

"Not really," Gloria argued. "We're going to explore the island during the day. Perhaps in the meantime, the investigators will be able to stumble on some clues and save us the trouble."

"Stop you from snooping," Paul snorted. "I guess I might as well save my breath. Don't forget to call me tomorrow. Allie and I are heading up to Dot's Restaurant for a late dinner before they close."

Gloria told Paul she loved him and then disconnected the call. She stared at the cell phone in her hand. Maybe Paul was right. She was getting a bad feeling about the killer, that there was something more to the murder than a simple drug deal gone bad.

It was something she would worry about tomorrow. All she wanted to do right now was crawl into bed and get some much needed rest.

***

Gloria spent the night tossing and turning. The bed was hard, the pillow flatter than a pancake and she was hot, although Brian had adjusted the thermostat for the mid-60's.

She could hear Brian shifting in the creaky bed across from hers and guessed he was having as much trouble sleeping as she, but then he was the one being investigated for Brodwell's murder. If she were in his shoes, she'd have trouble sleeping, too.

Finally, the first rays of morning light beamed in through the gap in the curtain and she climbed out of bed and tiptoed to the bathroom. Gloria had placed her overnight bag and a clean set of clothes in the bathroom the night before.

After she showered and dressed, she tiptoed into the living room. Brian was already up and had made a fresh pot of coffee.

"I'm sorry if I woke you."

"Nah." Brian yawned loudly. "I couldn't sleep. My bed is harder than the bunks in a jail cell."

Gloria frowned. "That's not funny."

"Yes, it is." He grinned. "Besides, I'm not worried about a stinky old jail cell. You're going to get me off the hook."

He grabbed his suitcase on the way to the bathroom while Gloria shuffled to the coffee pot and poured a cup. She opened the curtains and gazed out the window as she sipped the hot caffeine.

It was going to be a beautiful day for a bike ride and to explore the island of Nantucket. She made a mental note to find a local grocery store where they could purchase picnic supplies to take on their bike ride.

Brian emerged a short time later and refilled his coffee cup. “I don’t know about you but I’m starving. Last night on the bike ride back to the motel, I noticed a small café a short walk from here if you want to check it out.”

“Sure. While we’re at it, we need to find a grocery store to grab some picnic supplies.” It was still early and Brian and Gloria decided not to disturb the others. Instead, they took the short walk to the small café down on Main Street.

Brian held the door and waited for Gloria to step inside. The smell of freshly brewed coffee and cinnamon wafted to the door. She sniffed appreciatively. “It smells like cinnamon rolls.”

The sign near the door said ‘*seat yourself*’ so they wandered to a small corner table and settled in. The menu was limited, which was fine with Gloria. She settled on their pumpkin pancakes with a side of bacon while Brian decided on the lumberjack breakfast, complete with three eggs, hash browns, a small stack of pancakes, sausage and white toast.

"You really are hungry."

Brian reached for his cup of coffee. "I have a feeling you women are going to work me hard today. I need to fuel up."

The waitress returned a short time later with their food and she transferred it from her tray to the table. Gloria waited for her to finish setting the dishes on the table. "We're looking for a local store where we can pick up some picnic supplies. Can you recommend someplace?"

The girl tucked the empty tray under her arm. "Sure can. It's Olson's Deli four doors down. They don't open 'til ten or so, but they have a nice variety of homemade dishes including fried chicken, perfect for a picnic."

Gloria thanked the girl and waited until she had walked away before placing her napkin in her lap. They bowed their heads and Gloria prayed for a peaceful, stress-free day as well as a productive evening.

Brian reached for his fork and sawed off a piece of sausage patty. "While I was wide awake last night, I racked my brain, trying to remember if I was forgetting anything leading up to the time I discovered Brodwell's body inside the motel room."

"And?" Gloria reached for a slice of bacon.

"Looking back, there was something that seemed a little odd," he said. "Mr. and Mrs. Thornton left the pool area. I watched them climb into their sedan. They started to pull out of the parking lot when the car abruptly stopped. Libby Thornton darted out of the car and ran over to Brodwell, who was still sitting at one of the tables near the pool. I could've sworn she handed him something before heading back to the car and the Thorntons drove off."

Chapter 15

"You don't have any idea what she handed him?" Gloria asked.

"Not a clue, other than it was something small, but again, I was so far away I couldn't see."

Gloria bit her bacon and chewed thoughtfully. "Perhaps it was a key or a slip of paper, a note."

"He shoved his hand in his pocket right after she left," Brian said.

"The police would've found it," Gloria mused. "Which means it may have linked Brodwell to the Thorntons."

"I'm sure the police have already questioned them," Brian said.

"If David Thornton is friends with the local chief of police, I doubt the Thorntons are considered suspects."

Brian frowned. "They didn't have anything nice to say about me and I'm sure they said some things to the investigators, which is why I was questioned so extensively." He sucked in a deep breath. "Not to mention all the evidence points to me. Motive and opportunity."

Brian was right. It didn't look good. He was at the scene of the crime…opportunity. Motive was Brodwell's connection to Brian's fiancée.

Had Libby Thornton given Brodwell Andrea's room key, or maybe her phone number or address in Belhaven? It could have been any number of things.

Gloria pulled her cell phone from her purse, switched it on and flipped to the photos Dot had taken of the inside of the motel room. She tapped the screen and studied the pictures after sliding her reading glasses on.

The top of the dresser was crammed full of stuff and the picture slightly blurry. It was difficult to tell what was what, other than the unmistakable pill bottle containers. "I'm stumped. We'll have to wait until later tonight to see if we can glean any more clues from this Luke fellow."

They finished their breakfast and wandered out onto the sidewalk. Gloria glanced up and down the street before checking the time. "We still have some time to kill before the grocery store opens."

They strolled down the sidewalk and although Gloria was tempted to drag Brian into a few of the antique stores, she kept moving. Finally, he stopped and pointed at one of the stores. "Do you mind if we go in? I spotted some antique tools on one of the shelves."

"Of course." They headed inside and Brian made a beeline for the tools while Gloria wandered over to one of the display cases. Inside the display case was an old pocket watch.

She leaned forward and peered through the glass. On the front of the watch was a farm scene with a barn in the foreground. It reminded Gloria of her farm.

"May I help you?" A tall bookish man approached the back of the display case.

"I'm interested in the pocket watch, the one with the barn on it. Does the watch work?"

The man nodded as he slid the door of the case open and reached for the watch. "Yes. This piece came in yesterday. I've been admiring it myself." He handed her the vintage watch.

Gloria ran her finger over the top before pressing the clasp and opening the cover. Paul already owned a similar watch but the carving on the front was different. "How much is it?"

"Eighty-five bucks," the man said. "Should be more, but the chain isn't the original."

Gloria rubbed the sturdy chain. "I'll take it," she said impulsively, knowing Paul would be thrilled to have it and thrilled to know she'd been thinking of him.

The man wrapped it in tissue before placing it inside a small plastic bag. Gloria handed him her debit card and then followed him to the cash register near the back of the store.

She ran into Brian on her way to the check out. He was carrying an arm full of old tools and an antique brass doorknocker. "Let me help." Gloria reached for the doorknocker.

"I'm buying this for Andrea," Brian said as he handed it to her. "I figured she could find a place for it after I spit shine it."

"She'll love it," Gloria said. They made their way to the cash register and the clerk handed Gloria her card and bag.

She stepped off to the side to wait for Brian to pay for his treasures and then they wandered back onto the sidewalk. "That was fun," she said.

"I love shopping for antiques," Brian confessed. "Sometimes, I sneak off to the Belhaven flea market on Monday morning if the hardware store isn't busy."

Gloria remembered the knitting needles and yarn she found inside one of the hardware store drawers, not long after Brian's attack. "You're full of surprises." She kept mum about the discovery of the knitting needles, deciding that if, and when, he wanted to tell her about his hobby, he would.

They continued down the sidewalk toward Olson's Deli, which was now open and they wandered inside. Gloria's cell phone beeped. It was a text from Margaret, wondering where they were.

Gloria texted back that Brian and she had gotten up early and gone out for breakfast. She assured Margaret they would be back soon with the picnic supplies they were taking on the bicycle trip.

She offered to grab breakfast sandwiches for those who hadn't eaten yet, but Margaret told her they planned to pick something up on their way out. Lucy and Alice would be waiting for them at the motel but the others were leaving.

They made their way to the hot foods display case and ordered a large box of mixed fried chicken pieces, along with a large container of potato salad and a package of sweet rolls. Gloria grabbed a bag of potato chips and some cold sodas on the way to the checkout counter.

She added a disposable cooler to the purchases to keep the potato salad and sodas cold and then insisted she pay for the picnic supplies since Brian had bought dinner the night before.

After she finished paying, they made their way out of the store for the short walk back to the motel. Ruth's van was gone and Lucy and Alice's suite door was ajar.

Gloria tapped lightly and then pushed the door open with her elbow. "Knock, knock."

Lucy rushed over to grab the bag of food while Alice took the cold drinks and set them on the small table. "My goodness. Are you feeding a small army?"

"Better to have too much food than not enough." Gloria eased the other bag of food on the table, right next to the fried chicken.

"We rented a bike for Alice while you were gone." Lucy waved a piece of paper in the air. "I picked up a tourist map in the office and discovered a bike trail we can take."

Lucy spread the map out on her unmade bed and everyone gathered around as she outlined the bike route. It was a little more than five miles with a couple spots to stop along the way, if needed. They would end the ride at the lighthouse where they would have lunch.

It was manageable and since none of them had ridden for any length of time for years, it would be just enough so they weren't exhausted by the end of the ride.

Gloria quickly packed up the picnic supplies, splitting the food, drinks, sunscreen and bottled water between several backpacks.

Lucy led the parade of bikes and they coasted out of the parking lot.

“We’re going to swing by the Thornton’s hotel so Alice can try to talk to them,” Gloria reminded Lucy, who nodded her agreement.

The bike ride to the hotel was only a few short blocks. Brian, Lucy and Gloria waited out front while Alice climbed off her bike. She dropped the kickstand and removed her bike helmet. “Wish me luck.”

“You’re probably going to need it,” Brian muttered under his breath.

Alice disappeared inside the sliding doors.

“I give it a 50/50 chance of Alice finding out any new information,” Lucy predicted.

“Ninety ten,” Brian said.

"I'll go with the 50/50, too." Maybe it was wishful thinking on Gloria's part, but she hoped the Thorntons would be a little more forthcoming. After all, Brian would soon be their son-in-law.

Alice emerged a short time later and walked over to where they were waiting. Gloria could tell from the frown on her face it hadn't gone well.

"They weren't there?" Lucy asked.

"Oh, I find them all right," Alice said. "At first, they refuse to come down to the lobby to talk with me but then I guess they change their mind."

"And?" Gloria prompted.

"They say you brainwash Andrea and me."

"Me?" Gloria pointed at her chest.

"All of you," Alice said. "They say they hope we come to our senses." Her gaze shifted to Brian.

"What else?" Brian asked. "They said I killed Brodwell."

Alice shrugged uneasily. "Not in so many words. It no matter. They no help, but they still worry about Andrea and Mr. Brodwell's killer still on the loose." She made her way over to her bike and kicked up the kickstand. "We no worry about them. We solve this ourselves." Alice lifted her chin, a look of determination in her eyes.

"At least we know where we stand with them now," Lucy said. "Let's try not to dwell on them and enjoy our day." She led the group down the street toward the beginning of the bike trail.

Alice and Gloria rode behind Lucy, and Brian brought up the rear. Gloria insisted they all wear bike helmets since they were rusty riders and for Brian's sake because of his recent head injury. He didn't put up a fuss and Gloria was relieved.

The sun was bright with nary a cloud in the sky. The morning air was crisp and cool, and a light breeze blew off the water.

During the ride, Gloria mulled over Sean Brodwell's death. She was anxious to question "Luke" and wondered if he would give them some idea of why he had met with Sean Brodwell.

She also wondered what Libby Thornton had handed to Brodwell. Perhaps it was money. After all, he had checked out of the swanky Ocean View Resort and moved into the smaller, less luxurious Shady Cove Motel.

The four of them stopped at the corner of a busy intersection before hopping off their bicycles and walking them across the street.

The fresh air was invigorating and Gloria wished Paul could have been there. She hoped that one day the two of them could visit the quaint island to do some sightseeing as well as plan a deep sea-fishing excursion for Paul.

Lucy mentioned that Margaret had something planned for the following day but it would require a second vehicle.

They rounded a bend for the last leg of their ride. Gloria focused her attention on the bike path and the flow of vehicle traffic. Either the drivers didn't realize they were crowding the bike riders' space or they didn't care.

When they reached the park, the four of them walked the bikes to a small pavilion and parked them off to the side. After they unloaded the backpacks and set the food on the picnic table, they took turns using the restroom to wash up.

Gloria was the first to arrive back at the picnic table and Brian was right behind her. Lucy and Alice went to wash up. "You don't think it's possible the Thorntons gave Sean Brodwell money." She explained her theory of how he had checked out of the luxurious resort and checked into a smaller, cheaper motel several blocks away.

"Could be." Brian popped the top on an ice-cold can of Coke and took a big swig. He gazed thoughtfully out at the playground nearby. "You don't think she gave him a key to Andrea's room."

Gloria frowned. "That's crazy. What parent would do such a thing? I also don't understand why Andrea's parents filed a missing person's report if they suspected she intentionally left the island and returned to Belhaven."

Brian shrugged. "They're odd ducks, for sure."

Alice and Lucy returned and settled in at the picnic table. Gloria was starving. Her pancake breakfast was long gone.

They passed around the containers of fried chicken and potato salad, the rolls and then Gloria dumped a handful of chips onto the side of her paper plate. "Let's pray."

She let Brian pray. "Dear Heavenly Father. Thank you for this beautiful day. Thank you for this food. I also thank you for my friends, for those around me who are trying to help clear my name. Amen."

"And we ask that the killer is quickly uncovered," Gloria added. "Amen."

The picnic lunch hit the spot and they devoured the food. All that was left was a half bag of potato chips.

Gloria folded the top of the bag of chips and carefully eased it into her backpack. Something was nagging in the back of her mind and a feeling of impending doom swept over her.

She trailed behind the others as they headed toward the bicycles. Gloria eased the helmet onto her head and reached for the clasp. It was in that moment, she realized what had been bothering her. She spun on her heel and faced Brian.

"Andrea said her parents suspected she was returning to Belhaven. If they were determined to have her reconcile with Sean Brodwell, do you think Libby gave her daughter's home address to Sean so he could follow her to Michigan?"

Alice gasped. "Oh, I hope you wrong Miss Gloria."

Brian's expression grew grim. "Someone trashed Brodwell's motel room. They were looking for something."

"We need to figure out if police found anything in Brodwell's pants pocket," Lucy gasped.

"In the meantime, I'm going to call Andrea to tell her she needs to stay at the farm just in case someone followed her home." Gloria fumbled inside her backpack, searching for her cell phone.

Chapter 16

Andrea Malone could not shake the feeling she was being followed. It started right after she left her house early that morning. The feeling persisted as she ran her errands, stopping by the post office and the drug store. She also stopped by Dot's Restaurant to say "hello" to Johnnie Morris and Dot's husband, Ray, and to apologize for causing everyone so much grief.

Both men assured her it was fine and that if it hadn't been Andrea in trouble, it would've been something or someone else.

Andrea ordered Dot's specialty, the early bird breakfast platter, to go. After it was ready, she paid for the meal and then dropped it off in her pickup truck before heading to the last store on the corner of Main Street...Nails and Knobs, Brian's hardware store.

Andrea opened the door and stepped inside. Tears filled her eyes at the familiar aroma of cedar and pine-sol. The smells reminded her of Brian. She swallowed hard and forced herself to walk to the rear of the store.

Mark Clawson, Brian's new part-time employee, looked up from the counter when Andrea approached. "Hi Andrea. The rumor is true. You're back home while Brian, who set out to rescue his damsel in distress, is in Nantucket."

Andrea gave him a watery smile. "My foolish pride has managed to cause a lot of trouble," she admitted.

Mark shook his head. "No sense in beating yourself up over this. We all do things we later regret."

"Thanks. I appreciate your words of encouragement." Andrea glanced around the store. "Something looks different."

"Yeah, after Brian's accident and while you were gone, he decided to rearrange the store. He said something about better traffic flow. I think he was trying to stay busy myself."

They chatted for a few moments and Andrea glanced at her watch. "I left my breakfast in the truck. I better head home before it gets cold."

She waved good-bye and then headed out of the store. The eerie feeling of being followed had vanished and Andrea scolded herself for her overactive imagination. She picked up the pace as she headed to the truck where she climbed inside.

The smell of bacon filled the cab of the pickup truck and Andrea's mouth watered. She hadn't had much of an appetite in weeks, not since Brian's accident. She backed out of her parking spot and pulled onto the street. A catchy country song was playing on her favorite radio station and she turned it up as she sang along.

When she reached her private drive, she noticed the gate was ajar. "I could've sworn I shut the gate on my way out." Andrea hopped out of the truck, pushed the gate open and then climbed back inside before she eased the truck around the curve and up the drive.

Brutus, Andrea's black lab, bounded across the yard and met Andrea at the driver's side door.

"How on earth did you get out?" She had left Brutus in a small, gated area near the rear of the property so he wouldn't tear up her freshly planted flowers while she was gone.

Brutus tore off across the yard and Andrea reached inside the truck for her food and purse. The eerie sensation she was being watched returned with a vengeance.

Her scalp began to tingle. For a split second, she thought about climbing back into her pickup truck and high tailing it out of there. Instead, she reached inside her purse and pulled out her 9mm handgun.

Andrea held it in a tight grip as she eased along the hedge toward the front door. When she got there, she inserted her key in the front door to unlock it. She pushed the door open and took a small step forward. "Hello?"

Nothing looked out of place. *Andrea Malone, you need to get a grip.*

Andrea relaxed her shoulders and placed the bag of food on the floor inside the door. "I better corral that crazy dog," she muttered. "I wonder how he got out."

She backed out of the door, pulling it shut behind her and collided with a tall, looming figure who stood in the doorway, directly behind her.

***

"She's not answering," Gloria groaned. "You try," she told Brian.

Brian dialed Andrea's number and it went right to voice mail. "It went to voice mail."

Alice clasped her hands. "We have to do something. Miss Andrea might be in danger."

"I'll call Paul." Gloria quickly scrolled her phone list and dialed Paul's number.

"Hello?"

"Thank goodness you answered," Gloria said. "Andrea may be in trouble. There's a chance the guy who died was some sort of drug dealer unbeknownst to Andrea. Brian said Libby Thornton handed something to Brodwell minutes before he returned to his motel room, right before he was murdered."

"Okay," Paul said.

"Well, what if Libby Thornton, who admitted she figured Andrea left abruptly to return home, gave Brodwell Andrea's home address? The killer trashed Brodwell's motel room searching for something. If the killer searched Brodwell's pants pockets, the killer would've found whatever Libby had given him..."

Gloria tightened her grip on the phone. "I know it's a stretch, but I would feel much better if

Andrea stayed at the farm with you and Allie until we get home."

"You're right. Better safe than sorry, especially if this Brodwell was a drug dealer and someone had torn his motel room apart searching for something," Paul said. "I'll head over there in a couple minutes," he promised. "In the meantime, maybe you should give her a call."

"We already tried. It went right to voice mail."

"She could be out running errands. I'm on my way," Paul said. "I'll call you as soon as I track her down."

After they hung up, Gloria dropped her cell phone into her purse. "I won't be able to relax until Paul calls me back."

Brian's jaw tightened. "Me either. More than anything, I wish we were back home."

"Me too, Brian," Gloria said. "Me too."

Chapter 17

Paul Kennedy grabbed his car keys off the hook and reached for the doorknob. "I'll be back in a minute, Allie," he hollered into the back of the house.

He was convinced his wife had a sixth sense for trouble and if she thought Andrea might be in trouble, then Paul gave it a 50/50 chance that she was.

Paul had talked to Andrea the previous evening and, since Alice and Brian were both gone and there was no one around, he even asked if she would be more comfortable staying at the farm.

She'd insisted she would be fine and that Brutus was a reliable guard dog. She assured him he would be the first to know if she needed anything.

Paul climbed into his car, backed out of the driveway and pulled onto the road. He pressed hard on the gas pedal as he sped down the backroad toward the small town of Belhaven. The fact Andrea hadn't answered when both Gloria and Brian had called caused a small degree of concern.

When he reached town, he turned right and headed up the hill toward Lake Terrace where Andrea's stately home sat atop a large hill not far from the lake. Paul drove past the open gate and onto the drive before rounding the small curve.

He spotted Andrea's truck in the drive. The driver's side door was wide open. There was a four-door car parked behind it. Paul had never seen the vehicle before.

Andrea was nowhere in sight, although her dog, Brutus, was wandering around the backyard. He felt an unsettling in the pit of his stomach. Something wasn't right.

Paul parked on the other side of Andrea's truck. He reached inside his glove box and pulled out his revolver, checking to make sure it was loaded before he climbed out of his car.

As he passed by Andrea's open truck door, he looked inside. There was no trace of Andrea or her belongings. He continued walking toward the house and as he got close, he noticed the front door was ajar.

Paul slipped along the edge of the hedge as he hurried toward the house.

When he reached the front porch, he heard Andrea's muffled voice and then the tinkle of laughter. Paul loosened his grip on the gun. "Hello?"

He peered through the open door and gazed into the front foyer. "Andrea?"

Andrea emerged from the dining room, a bright smile on her face. "Hi Paul."

A tall, broad-shouldered man followed behind Andrea. Paul had never seen him before. "Hello." He nodded at the man.

"Paul, this is Pierce Wright. He works for my parents in New York. They sent him here to check on me."

"Pierce, this is Paul Kennedy, Gloria's husband."

Paul extended his hand. "I do believe I've heard Andrea mention your name before, all good of course. It's a pleasure to finally meet you."

Pierce took Paul's hand in a firm grasp. "Same here. I've heard many good things about you."

Paul released his grasp and turned to Andrea. "Brian and Gloria were concerned for your safety and wanted me to come by to check on you since you weren't answering your phone."

"Oh!" Andrea reached in her back pocket and pulled out her cell phone. "Whoops! I had the volume down. Shame on me. I better give them a call."

Andrea stepped out onto the porch and Paul turned to Pierce. "I didn't want to scare Andrea but Brian and Gloria were concerned someone may have followed Andrea to Belhaven."

Pierce nodded gravely. "The Thorntons were concerned, as well. As soon as they found out Andrea was back in Belhaven, they booked my flight. I'm here until Mr. Sellers and Alice return or Mr. Brodwell's killer is apprehended."

"That will ease a lot of minds," Paul said. The men made small talk until Andrea reappeared. "I was able to reach Brian. He was with Gloria. They're both relieved Pierce is here." She reached over and slipped her arm through Pierce's arm. "It's like having my own personal bodyguard."

Pierce tugged on the edge of Andrea's long locks. "So you're giving others the same gray hairs you've given me over the years."

"I'll head on out of here and give you two a chance to catch up." Paul briefly hugged Andrea and turned to go. "Don't hesitate to call if you need anything."

Paul climbed into his car, backed out of the drive and pulled onto the road. He called Gloria on the way back to the farm.

"I'm glad Pierce is there with Andrea," Gloria said when he answered. "That makes me feel so much better."

"Me too," Paul agreed. "He seems like a nice fellow and Andrea appears to adore him."

"They're close," Gloria said. "Just like Andrea and Alice."

They chatted for several moments, until Paul reached the farm. “I’m home now. Is there anything else I need to do…any other damsel in distress I need to rescue before I head inside and make lunch?” he teased.

“No, but you’ll be the first to know. We’re heading back to Barnacle Bill’s restaurant later today to try to track down this Luke fellow.”

“Don’t go alone,” Paul said.

“I won’t. I think everyone is going,” Gloria said. “I’ll call you later.” She thanked her husband one more time, telling him how much she loved him and missed him before disconnecting the line.

It was a short bike ride back to Craggy Manor. Ruth’s van was parked in the same spot it had occupied previously and the four of them headed to Lucy, Alice and Margaret’s suite to drop off their things.

No one was inside so they headed to the other suite, the one that Dot, Ruth and Rose occupied. No one answered when Gloria knocked so they swung by Brian and Gloria's suite to drop off their backpacks and park the bikes inside.

"They might be down by the pool," Alice said.

Sure enough, the rest of the gang was hanging out by the pool, soaking up the mid-afternoon sunshine. Margaret was swimming in the pool.

Gloria wandered to the edge and bent down to dip her fingers in the water. "Isn't the water cold?"

"Nope. It's a heated pool. The water is perfect. You should join me."

"I forgot my swimsuit." Gloria shook her head.

"I bring mine. I love to swim." Alice turned on her heel and headed out of the courtyard, returning moments later wearing a bright floral one-piece bathing suit and carrying a room towel.

"Well, look at you," Gloria grinned. "You're like a bright ray of beautiful sunshine."

"I come prepared," Alice said.

"You sure did." Rose stuck a hand on her hip and gazed at the sparkling pool. "Now I wouldn't get into that pool if you gave me a brand new Cadillac."

"Really?" Gloria asked. "You don't like pools?"

"No ma'am." Rose shook her head. "I can't swim and am deathly afraid of anything but the bathtub."

"I'll have to remember that," Alice quipped.

Rose frowned.

Gloria patted Rose's arm. "She's kidding." She turned to Alice. "You are kidding, right?"

Alice smiled and winked before she dove into the pool and came up on the other side.

Alice and Margaret frolicked in the water while Brian excused himself. He said the bike ride had given him a dull headache and he was going to lie down for a while.

"I hope I didn't cause him to over exert himself," Gloria fretted. "Sometimes I get so wound up, I don't think."

Dot shaded her eyes, reached over and patted Gloria's arm. "I'm sure he'll be fine. It's easy to forget how badly he was injured."

"It can't help he's being questioned in Brodwell's murder," Lucy added. "It has to be troubling him."

"Or the fact his fiancée is hundreds of miles away and he's here," Gloria said. "At least Pierce is there to watch over her."

"Pierce." Ruth shifted in her lounge chair. "The name sounds familiar."

"Pierce is the Thornton's driver and full-time employee. He's worked for them for many moons." Gloria explained to the others her feeling that someone might have followed Andrea to Belhaven.

She told them how they'd tried to reach Andrea and when they couldn't, Gloria asked Paul to run by her place. "Thankfully, the Thorntons were concerned, as well, because Pierce said as soon as they found out Andrea was back in Belhaven, they purchased his plane ticket and he headed to Michigan."

"You don't suppose Andrea's parents are part of some drug ring and they think their only child is now a target?" Ruth asked.

"I don't know what to think," Gloria said. "It looks suspicious, at least to me."

"Me too," Dot said.

Alice and Margaret finally emerged from the pool and spread their towels on nearby lounge chairs after drying off.

Margaret adjusted her chair before settling in and closing her eyes. "Ah. This is the life. I haven't been on vacation in years."

"What about our cruise?" Lucy asked.

"That was part vacation and part crisis," Margaret insisted. "I mean what are the chances of being on board a cruise ship that's been hijacked?"

"Ninety-five to ninety-nine percent odds if you're with Gloria Rutherford-Kennedy," Dot joked.

Gloria cleared her throat and frowned at her friend.

"Ah, the good ole days," Ruth said. "Speaking of that, I forwarded the video footage of Dot snapping those photos of the inside of Brodwell's motel room and the police chasing after her."

"That's not right," Dot declared.

"Whew! You shoulda seen the look on your face when you realized the cops were coming after you." Ruth chuckled.

Despite Dot's repeated insistence that Ruth erase the video footage, the others unanimously voted to view the footage later that evening.

"It's only because we need to study it for more clues," Ruth assured their friend.

Gloria adjusted the arms of her chair so she could recline on the lounger when the sight of a police cruiser pulling into the parking lot caught her attention. "Now what?"

Chapter 18

Gloria had a sinking feeling the officer was there to talk to Brian and after a brief stop at the front office, she watched as the man crossed the parking lot and began knocking on the door of their motel room.

A second car, this one a sedan with tinted windows, pulled up and parked next to the police cruiser. A man stepped out of the vehicle and headed to the motel room to join the uniformed officer.

The motel room door opened and then the men disappeared inside. Gloria said a silent prayer they were there to tell Brian they had cleared his name and he was free to leave.

Somehow, it seemed too easy and her suspicions were correct. Brian returned to the pool area a short time later, a grim expression on his face. He opened the gate and stepped inside.

"The investigator, Detective Flint, had a few more questions." Brian eased onto one of the empty lounge chairs and faced the others. "Judging by his questions and the tone of his voice, I have a hunch investigators don't have any other suspects and plan to pin Brodwell's murder on me...and they seem to be in a big hurry to do it."

"Who was the other guy?" Gloria asked. "It looked like another officer in street clothes."

"Believe it or not, that was the chief of police. I guess it must be a slow day for crime on the island." His shoulders sagged. "I had motive and opportunity. They know all about Andrea and me, the reason I'm here and the fact Brodwell had been the last one seen with Andrea."

"The chief is also friends with the Thorntons," Lucy said. "Doesn't that seem odd for him to become personally involved in an investigation?"

"Maybe he's doing some friends a favor," Ruth said.

"Did you ask about the note?" Gloria asked. "Did you tell them the Thorntons met with Sean Brodwell just before his death and how Libby Thornton handed something to Brodwell right before he returned to his motel room?"

"I did." Brian nodded. "Of course, they aren't going to tell me anything, but I could've sworn I saw a flicker of surprise in the investigator's eyes when I told him."

"Don't worry Brian," Gloria said. "I have a feeling we're on the right track with this Luke fellow. He knows something."

"I wonder if the investigators have tried talking to Andrea yet," Ruth said.

"With everything that has gone on, I forgot to ask her. I'll ask Paul when I call him tonight," Gloria said.

They lounged by the pool for a while longer. Alice and Margaret took another dip in the pool before the group headed back to their rooms to get ready for dinner.

Gloria hoped to arrive at the restaurant a little early so she could walk the marina to see if she could spot the Fathom, the mysterious yacht, and perhaps snap a couple photos of it.

The group agreed to meet in Margaret, Lucy and Alice's suite since the lingering odor of garlic and Rose's candle hung in the air. The trio claimed they could no longer smell it but every time Gloria stepped inside, her stomach churned.

Lucy was the first one ready to go, and she plopped down next to Gloria on the small sofa in the living room.

Gloria glanced at her friend's outfit, a pair of fire engine red capris and a sleeveless white button down blouse. She did a double take as she peered at Lucy's heart-shaped earrings. "Those earrings look familiar."

Lucy reached up and touched one of the dangling hearts. She grinned. “I wondered if you would remember. I wore them to Daniel Malone’s funeral.”

Gloria shifted to the side. “The mini cameras. You’re wearing the mini camera earrings.”

Click. “Yep. I just took your picture.”

Ruth, who had been sitting in front of her laptop checking to make sure she had the video footage of the police officers pursuit of Dot, shoved her chair back and wandered across the room. “Phantom X spy earrings from Del Babba’s Online Mart.” She leaned forward for a closer inspection of the earrings. “I had my eye on them a few months back but never bought them.”

“Why not?” Gloria asked. “I would think spy camera earrings would go nicely with your spy equipment collection.”

“Too girly.” Ruth wrinkled her nose. “I didn’t care for the hearts. Now if they had them in say a postage stamp or the shape of the Michigan mitten, I might've bought them."

Gloria eased off the couch. Ruth squeezed in next to Lucy and they discussed the merits of the mini spy cameras. "I plan to take some pictures of Barnacle Bill and the mysterious Luke," Lucy said. "I have it set up to download right to my phone so we can transfer the pictures from my phone to my email and study them later."

"Smart. Very smart." Ruth nodded her head in approval. "Meanwhile, I can set the van's surveillance cameras to record the front entrance while we're inside on recon. I plan to record some audio as well." Ruth slapped the top of her leg before popping off the sofa. "It looks like we have all our bases covered. Time for me to go get ready."

She hurried out of the room and Gloria waited until the door closed. "I swear Ruth was a spy in another life."

Lucy nodded. "I'm more of a weapons gal myself, but it doesn't hurt to activate the entire arsenal. We need all the help we can get."

Brian, who had been sitting on the couch scrolling through television channels, stood. "I think I'll go change too."

Brian exited the motel room. Gloria watched as he passed by the large picture window out front, leaving only Lucy, Margaret and Gloria in the living room. "I hate to say this in front of Brian, but do you think Andrea's parents are involved in Brodwell's murder?"

"We don't know them that well," Margaret said. "Andrea hasn't lived at home with her parents in years."

"Alice lived with them for decades. Surely she would've said something if she suspected her former employers were cold-blooded killers," Gloria said.

"True," Lucy agreed.

Gloria wandered out of the suite and let herself into the one Brian and she shared. She sat on the edge of the sofa and stared at the blank television screen. No loving parent would deliberately put his or her only child's life in danger.

Based on what Brian had said, the investigating officer seemed surprised when Brian told him Libby Thornton had given something to Brodwell and he had shoved it in his front pants pocket before making his way to his motel room.

It meant someone had checked the dead man's pockets…or he'd emptied them before his demise. Gloria couldn't wait to hear what Andrea's parents had to say when Andrea asked them about her mother handing something off to Brodwell.

It would be the perfect setup to get rid of Brian, which for the life of her, Gloria couldn't understand. Brian, a former circuit court judge and successful businessman, would make any in-law proud.

Gloria reminded herself the Thorntons were an odd couple, to say the least. Perhaps they hadn't liked Brodwell as much as they let on. They saw their opportunity to get rid of the men in Andrea's life, one by murder and the other by pinning the murder on Brian.

Andrea's mother was a retired doctor. Perhaps she'd gotten hooked on prescription drugs and now needed a drug dealer to keep her supplied.

Certainly, the authorities had questioned the Thorntons, although Gloria remembered hearing the Thorntons were friends with Nantucket's chief of police.

Brian emerged from the bathroom and headed to the kitchenette while Gloria traded places and made her way into the bathroom.

She hoped they would get a break tonight at Barnacle Bill's Seafood Restaurant. If Andrea was right and Sean had met with this mysterious Luke before his death, the man might hold the key to solving the murder.

There was only one way to find out. Gloria finished freshening up and spritzed some of her favorite perfume on both wrists and neck before emerging from the bathroom. "It's time to shift this investigation into high gear."

Chapter 19

Barnacle Bill's was a hopping place at 4:50 p.m. on a Wednesday afternoon. Ruth had to circle the parking lot twice before she finally found a spot she deemed the perfect location for not only setting up a visual and audio surveillance, but one that would decrease the chances of someone dinging the side of her precious van.

"I still don't get it," Lucy said as she hopped out of the back of the van. "I would think you would want to find out if your van is bullet proof, that the company who supplied you with their product would want you to try it." She was still hoping to take a shot at the van with her handgun. So far, Ruth was not on board.

"They do," Ruth hedged. "It's part of the agreement but I still have a little time." She patted her steering wheel lovingly. "It's just that she looks so pristine, so flawless, I'm having a hard time bringing myself to seriously think about it."

She turned the engine off and reached for the door handle. "When I'm ready, rest assured, Lucy, you'll be the first person I call."

The group exited the van and made their way to the end of the line of patrons who were waiting to get inside the restaurant.

When they reached the front of the line, they all squeezed in together. The hostess was the same one who had seated them during their last visit. She smiled when she recognized the large group. "Would you like to sit by the window again?"

"Yes." Gloria nodded and then realized they would need to be closer to the bar area where it was rumored "Luke" hung out. "I'm sorry. I changed my mind." She pointed to a large table to the right of the bar. "Can we have that one instead?"

"Sure." The girl waved them forward. "Follow me." She led them to a large table adjacent to the bar and placed a stack of menus on the edge of the table. "Your server will be right with you. Tonight is our all-you-can-eat shrimp."

"Thanks." Gloria pulled out her chair. It faced the bar and gave her an unobstructed view of the entire area. She settled in and immediately began studying the customers seated there.

Behind the bar was a tall, gray haired man with a weathered face. He tipped his head back and began laughing loudly as he pounded his fist on the bar top. "I think you're in need of another brew, my friend." The man reached under the counter, pulled out a frosted mug, filled it with beer from the tap in front of him and slammed it on the bar.

Gloria leaned forward. "My guess is he's Barnacle Bill."

Lucy, who was sitting next to Gloria, nodded. "I think you're right."

The server arrived moments later and jotted down their drink order. The young man recommended the Nantucket lemonade, explaining it consisted of ginger ale, lemonade, cranberry juice and fresh lime juice. Gloria decided to try it. Lucy ordered it, as well.

Margaret opted for Billy's Bodacious Brew and claimed it was all in the name of research.

After their server returned with their drink order, they placed their dinner order. Everyone agreed the shrimp special was too good a deal to pass up.

Gloria ordered the breaded shrimp as well as the wood-fired shrimp. After the server jotted their orders on his pad, Gloria reached for her glass of lemonade and took a sip. It was the perfect combination of tart and bubbly with a hint of sweet. She made a mental note to ask for the recipe since she thought Paul would enjoy it, too.

"Huh." Brian nodded his head toward the restaurant entrance. "I guess everyone on the island heads to Barnacle Bill's for the all-you-can-eat-shrimp."

Gloria followed his gaze. She watched as two men followed the hostess across the restaurant. "Who is that?"

"Detective Flint and Chief of Police Grobe," Brian said.

She watched while the hostess seated them at a corner table that faced the water before she turned her attention to the lively character behind the bar. He seemed to know everyone as he made his way along the back of the bar, chatting with the customers. The guests came and went, and each time a new male saddled up to the bar, Gloria studied the man, wondering if he was Luke.

The food arrived and after she silently prayed, she reached for her fork. A man eased behind her, bumping the back of her chair and Gloria slid the chair forward.

"Sorry ma'am. It's a tight squeeze. I didn't mean to bump your chair."

Gloria gazed up and into a set of the deepest blue eyes she'd ever seen, except for Brian's eyes. She smiled and nodded. "No problem."

The man continued to ease his way to the bar and climbed onto the empty barstool at the end.

The bartender approached the man. "Well, if it isn't my pal Smooth Hand Luke," he said in a loud voice. "I was beginnin' to think you weren't going to make it tonight."

"You know I haven't missed a Wednesday shrimp special in years, Bill," the man said as he swiveled in his chair.

Brian, whose back was to the bar, swung around to study the man. His jaw tightened and

Gloria hoped he wouldn't do anything to cause the man to become suspicious. She cleared her throat in an attempt to catch Brian's attention.

Brian's eyes met Gloria's eyes and he slowly nodded as he nonchalantly spun back around and reached for his glass of Coke.

Bill and Luke discussed the weather forecast and the condition of the seas. Finally, the conversation shifted and Luke lowered his voice as he leaned forward. They spoke in low voices.

"I'll be right back." Bill stepped to the side to wait on others at the bar. Another bartender took his place as he eased a heaping plate of shrimp in front of Luke.

Luke ate his food and drank his beer in silence. Bill made his way over as Luke finished his food. "That's all you're gonna eat?"

"I'm not very hungry," Luke replied. "Had to stop by the mainland earlier today to take care of some business and while I waited, I ate a big lunch."

Luke reached into his front pocket and pulled out a wad of bills.

Lucy's eyes widened. "We need to do something," she whispered. "I think he's getting ready to leave." She shoved her chair back, hopped out of her seat and darted around the table as she approached the bar.

Gloria watched as Lucy eased in next to Luke and then smiled at him. He smiled back as he wedged several bills under his empty beer mug.

Lucy began fiddling with her spy camera earring and Gloria's heart stopped when the man leaned forward for a closer look at the heart-shaped earring.

Cool-as-a-cucumber Lucy twisted the earring so the man had a closer look before leaning slightly back and reaching for her left earring to take pictures of the other section of the bar.

They chatted for several more moments and when Bill wandered over, Lucy turned her attention to him. He poured a beer and slid it across the counter. Lucy reached inside her purse to pull out her wallet. Luke motioned her to stop.

Lucy batted her eyes at Luke and then said something to Bill before she took a step back, grabbed the beer and made her way back to their table.

"I didn't know you liked beer," Gloria said.

"I don't." Lucy set it on the table and slid it toward Margaret. "But I had to come up with some excuse to head to the bar."

"Thanks." Margaret reached for the handle. "I wasn't going to order another one, but waste not, want not." She shrugged.

Gloria deliberately turned the conversation to the weather, keeping an eye on the bar as she nibbled on one of her shrimp. After they finished eating and Luke was still hanging out at the bar, having ordered another beer, the group exited the restaurant and headed to the van.

"Time for a stakeout," Ruth said as she clicked the key fob and unlocked the van doors. Everyone climbed inside. Lucy, Gloria and Brian sat on the floor since there weren't enough seats for everyone.

"I'm hot." Rose reached inside the storage compartment, grabbed a folded newspaper tucked inside and began fanning her face.

"Me too," Dot said.

Ruth started the van and turned the air conditioner on high. "So what did this Smooth Hand Luke have to say? He was flirting with you."

"Oh my gosh!" Lucy shook her head. "He wanted to take me back to his boat."

"Yacht," Margaret corrected.

"Yacht," Lucy said. "He said he was in love with my red hair. It reminded him of his last girlfriend, who fell off the side of his yacht somewhere between here and Martha's Vineyard a couple years ago and drowned. They never found her body. He wanted to give me a tour. I didn't know what to say. What if he planned to murder me and toss my body overboard?"

Alice shivered. "Why would he wanna tell a complete stranger something like that? That's creepy."

"I agree, although it may have been useful to have taken a peek at the inside the yacht in case there were any clues," Gloria said. "Anything else?"

"Yeah. He told me his yacht's name was *Fathom* and he called the man behind the bar, the older man, Bill."

Lucy continued. "I think I got some great close ups of him and the other customers at the bar. We can study them later. I was so nervous when Luke leaned in to check out my earrings, I thought I was gonna pass out."

"I was watching you, Lucy. I never would've suspected you were nervous," Gloria said.

Ruth, whose eyes never left the entrance to the restaurant, scrambled out of the driver's seat. "Well lookie who just arrived."

Gloria shifted her gaze and caught a glimpse of Libby and David Thornton as they walked inside Barnacle Bill's Seafood Restaurant.

Ruth wiggled past Gloria and crawled to the back. "I gotta adjust the FQ cameras." She unfolded her makeshift chair and pressed the buttons on the side monitor.

Gloria scooched past the bench seat and eased in behind Ruth as she studied the screen. There was a clear as a bell view of the interior of the restaurant.

Ruth shifted the dial and the camera zoomed in.

"I had no idea you could do that."

"This is the first chance I've had to use it." Ruth chewed her lower lip as she slowly eased the dial to the left. "Keep an eye out. Let me know if you see the Thorntons." The camera slowly panned the restaurant, starting near the floor-to-ceiling windows that faced the water. The place was packed.

"I don't see them," Gloria said. "There are too many people."

Ruth eased the dial to the left and began another perimeter visual of the interior of the restaurant.

Lucy, who was closest, leaned over Ruth's left shoulder. When the camera reached the bar area, Lucy pointed at the screen. "Wait! I see them. Their backs are to us and they're sitting at the bar."

"Right next to Smooth Hand Luke," Gloria said.

Chapter 20

"I have an idea." Lucy grabbed Rose's hand and pulled her toward the side door.

"Oh mercy, me." Rose attempted to pull her hand away. "Where you takin' me Lucy?"

"You'll see." Lucy flung the door open and dragged a reticent Rose with her. "I don't want to be alone with Luke and I know for certain the Thorntons have never met you since you and Johnnie moved to Belhaven after their last visit."

"Good luck," Gloria hollered through the door before Lucy slammed it shut.

Lucy and Rose hurried past the restaurant and over to the boat slips.

"I am deathly afraid of water," Rose's eyes widened. "I can't swim."

"You won't have to," Lucy said. "If Luke shows up, pretend to be interested in seeing his yacht or don't say anything at all. I'll do the talking."

"This is too much excitement."

"You wanted to join the infamous Garden Girls in this fun-filled adventure, so now you get a first-hand taste of the action," Lucy said. "Let's wander up and down the slips. I'll snap a few pictures with my earrings. If Luke doesn't show up before we finish, we'll leave."

"I hope he doesn't," Rose muttered under her breath as she eyed the murky waters.

Warped deck boards jutted up and the women cautiously made their way down the dock. Many of the boats, mostly the fishing boats, had at least one person on board and Lucy gave a friendly wave as the women slowly made their way to the end.

They finished inspecting the first row and headed to the second strip of slips where the large ferryboat was tied up off to the side. "You rode over here on the ferry." Lucy pointed to the ferryboat.

"But I didn't have to look at the water or get too close." Rose shaded her eyes against the setting sun and surveyed the calm waters. "It's pretty from a distance, I'll give you that."

They began the slow walk along the final set of slips when they ran into Luke coming from the other direction. "Didja' change yer mind and decide to take a look at my yacht?" He leaned in close, invading Lucy's personal space. She took a step back.

Luke belched and a burst of beer breath blew out of his lips. He teetered ever so slightly. Lucy wondered how many of Billy's bodacious brews the man had consumed. She shoved the thought aside. "We don't want to be a bother." She pointed to Rose. "My friend, Rose, wanted to take a closer look at the boats. She loves the water."

Rose cleared her throat but remained silent.

"Follow me." Luke waved them forward and they trailed behind as he swaggered down the dock. He stopped abruptly in front of a vessel. It looked almost identical to the yachts on either side. "This here is my love. I named 'er Fathom." He grabbed a wooden side post and stepped off the dock and onto the back of the yacht.

Luke reached back and offered Lucy his hand. She hesitated for a fraction of a second before slipping her hand in his and quickly hopping aboard.

Rose stood frozen on the dock, her eyes wide as she stared at the water. She took a step back.

"Hop aboard." Luke motioned her forward and reached out his hand. Rose gave Lucy a death look before extending her hand. Luke yanked a reluctant Rose onto the vessel.

"Whoo!" Rose's arms flailed wildly when her feet hit the deck. "This boat is rockin'.".

Luke snorted. “Yes ma’am. That’s because it’s a yacht and it’s in the water.”

Lucy attempted to divert attention from Rose’s growing pasty complexion to her surroundings. “This is spacious,” she complimented.

“It’s larger than a cuddy cabin,” Luke explained. “I have a small galley kitchen with a living area off to one side and a separate bedroom. This beaut also boasts a full-size shower in the bath. Let me give you a personal tour.” He lowered his eyelids seductively.

Lucy’s eyes widened. “I...uh.”

Luke slipped his arm around Lucy’s waist and whisked her forward.

Lucy shot Rose, who stood firmly planted near the back of the yacht, a terrified glance.

Rose shook her head. “I’ll wait for you out here.”

“I’ll be back in a minute.” Lucy gave Luke a quick glance. *What have I gotten myself into?*

Luke led Lucy to the galley kitchen. It was small but featured all the comforts of home. There was a half fridge with freezer, a two-burner stove and small oven. The sink was a single bowl but deep. There was even ample counter space. Lucy was impressed. "This is nice."

Luke leered. "Perhaps you'd like to join me for a moonlit boat ride."

Lucy remembered Luke mentioning during their brief conversation at the bar how his last girlfriend had fallen overboard and her body never found. She shook her head. "I'm sorry but I can't."

Luke led her to a door. He opened the door and stepped inside. It was the bedroom.

Lucy stood in the doorway, certain that if she stepped inside, flirtatious Luke would toss her atop the bed. Instead, she gripped the doorframe and kept her distance.

On both the left and right hand walls were large cabinets. Lucy reached out to touch one of the closet handles.

Luke lunged forward and slapped her hand. "You can't look in there!" he shouted abruptly.

Lucy snatched her hand back. "I didn't mean to pry."

Luke's voice softened. "I didn't mean to yell. I...the inside of the cabinets are a mess and I'm afraid if you opened them up, things would come flying out." He placed his hand under Lucy's elbow and steered her out of the bedroom.

They took a quick peek at the bathroom on their way up the steps where Rose sat perched on the edge of a cushioned bench near the back of the yacht, inches away from the boat dock.

Rose stood. "I must have eaten something bad. I'm feeling a little under the weather."

"We should go." Lucy hurried to Rose's side before she turned back. "Thank you for the tour of your boat...yacht," she told Luke. "Do you live on it?"

"Yes, ma'am." Luke nodded. "I do business between the islands and mainland. Keeps me busy. The only day of the week I'm here in Nantucket is on Wednesday. Maybe I can take you to dinner next week?" he asked hopefully.

"No, I'm sorry. I think we'll be heading back home by then," she said.

"Where's home?" Luke asked.

"Michigan," Rose blurted out.

"Minnesota," Lucy said at the same time. She shot Rose an uneasy glance. "I was born in Michigan but the weather is too nice there so I moved to Minnesota. I like lots and lots of subzero temperatures. Christmas isn't the same without frigid temps." She laughed uneasily.

"Huh."

"We better head out," Lucy took a step up. "Thanks again for the tour, Luke."

She waited for Rose to reach the safety of the dock before giving Luke a small wave. They hurried back to shore. Neither of them spoke until they reached the shoreline.

Lucy didn't dare look back but could feel Luke's eyes bore into her. She shivered. "He's hiding something on that boat...yacht."

"Bodies?" Rose asked.

"I don't know," Lucy said. "I don't think his bedroom closets are deep enough to hold bodies." She caught sight of Ruth's van parked in the same spot. "Good. They didn't leave us behind."

Gloria opened the door and Rose and Lucy climbed in the back. "Well? I saw Smooth Hand Luke head down the dock so I figured he caught up with you."

"He gave me a tour of his yacht. He said he lives on it and does his business on the other islands plus the mainland. He's only in Nantucket on Wednesday evenings and heads out first thing Thursday morning." Lucy swept a loose strand of hair from her eyes. "Thank goodness."

Lucy scooched to the other side of the van so there would be room for Rose. "I tried to open one of his bedroom closets during the tour and he freaked out."

Ruth eased the van into drive and pulled out of the parking spot. "We watched as a very nervous Libby and David Thornton exited the restaurant not long after Luke. I recorded the whole thing. We can study the tape when we get back to the motel."

Brian shifted in his seat. "You think Luke is a drug dealer, his deal with Sean went bad and he murdered him?"

"Maybe it's Bill Harding, the restaurant owner," Margaret said.

"Or they're partners," Dot added.

"What if Luke is a hitman and the Thorntons paid him to kill Sean," Gloria mused.

"But they liked Sean," Alice said.

"We need to go over all of our surveillance, audio and Lucy's photos," Ruth said. "Were you able to get some good shots of the inside of his yacht?"

"Oh my gosh!" Lucy reached up and touched her earring. "I was so nervous, I forgot to take pictures. What kind of sleuth am I?"

"A great one." Gloria reached over and patted her shoulder. "Don't worry Lucy. We should have enough on tape and audio, not to mention the pictures you took inside the restaurant, to sift through and find some clues."

"I hope so." Lucy brightened. "Hey Ruth! Make a pit stop at a convenience store on the way back to the motel. We'll need some popcorn and munchies to snack on while we're watching the videos."

Chapter 21

The group assembled in the tidiest, non-odiferous suite of the three...Brian and Gloria's suite. Ruth was one of the last to arrive. She swung the door open, dragging a large piece of luggage behind her.

She eased the backpack she was wearing off her shoulders and handed it to Brian, who was holding the door. "Be careful when you open this up. There's a relay box inside. I need it to transfer the files on my computer to the projector screen," she explained.

Brian unzipped the front of the backpack, pulled out a compact black box and placed it on the table.

"I'll pop the popcorn while you set up." Lucy grabbed the bag of goodies from the chair and headed to the kitchenette's microwave, tucked away in the corner of the suite.

Ruth eased the piece of luggage onto the carpeted floor, snapped the locks and lifted the lid.

Gloria peeked over her shoulder. "What is all of this?"

Ruth glanced up and then turned her attention to the task at hand. "It's a portable projector screen and tripod. It's not as nice as the one I have at home, but when you're traveling, this'll do in a pinch."

Margaret crossed the room. She leaned over and peered into the case. "Ruth Carpenter. I declare I have now seen it all."

Ruth's brow furrowed as she unsnapped the clasps on a large round cylinder. "Grab the other end," she told Margaret.

Margaret dropped to her knees and gently pulled on one side of the half cylinder while Ruth pulled the other. A large, white screen appeared. "This should do it," Ruth said. "Click the button on top to lock the screen in place."

"That is so cool." Lucy had finished popping the first bag of popcorn. She opened it up and grabbed a handful as she stared at the projector screen. "Where did you get this?"

"I found it on clearance on the internet and figured someday it might come in handy." Ruth scooted over to the case, reached inside and pulled out a set of poles. In no time, she had assembled a tripod. "Where should we put it?"

"Over here." Dot shifted the small dinette table out of the way to clear a spot.

Ruth centered the portable projector on the tripod and carried it across the room. She placed her hands on her hips and studied her handiwork. "Perfect."

Alice, who was the last to arrive, wandered into the suite. "What is that?"

"Ruth's portable projector and screen," Gloria said. "We don't have enough seats. Let's go grab a couple extra chairs from next door." Lucy, Margaret, Dot and Rose headed next door and returned, each carrying a chair.

They arranged the seats in a semi-circle so everyone had an unobstructed view of the screen.

"Ruth, you're a genius," Dot said.

Ruth's faced turned red. "Aww shucks, it ain't nothing."

"Don't sell yourself short, Ruth. This is awesome," Gloria said.

With the projector in place, Ruth settled in at the small table to begin downloading the files and setting up the relay box to project the files to the big screen. "I think I've got it."

Alice pulled the curtains shut and turned off the lights before taking her place next to Lucy.

"We'll start at the beginning with the footage of the motel room before Sean Brodwell's body was removed." It took a few moments for Ruth to adjust the footage so that it was clear.

The audio was garbled, except for the brief mention of drugs. The only thing they could hear were muffled voices, shoes shuffling and an occasional car as it passed by on the street out front.

For the most part, it was uneventful and Gloria's eyelids began to grow heavy. She nodded off at one point and jerked awake, hoping no one noticed. "I didn't see anything."

"Me either." Lucy ripped open the top of a snack size bag of peanut M&M's, poured a handful into her hand and then tossed them into her mouth.

"Let's move onto Dot's impromptu police pursuit," Ruth teased.

They all watched as Dot strolled across the motel parking lot. You could almost read Dot's mind as she abruptly stopped in front of Sean Brodwell's motel room and peered through the window before she pulled her cell phone from her purse.

She glanced behind her before she lifted the phone and angled it toward the window.

Everyone chuckled and Dot covered her eyes as she spun around and tore down the sidewalk at breakneck speed. She disappeared around the corner. Two uniformed officers, who were in hot pursuit, followed behind.

Ruth stopped the video when it got to the part where Ruth and Gloria ran past the front of the van as they followed Dot and the officers around the corner and out of sight.

Brian grinned and gave Dot a gentle hug. "Thanks for taking one for the team…for me, Dot."

"You're welcome, Brian." She lifted her chin and gave the giggling group a haughty gaze. "That's what friends are for."

"You're right," Gloria nodded. "That's what friends are for."

Next up were the pictures Dot took before the officers' foot pursuit. The first one was a blur. The second shot was the clearest and showed the pillow, the unmade bed and a section of the dresser.

Ruth tapped the keyboard and the top of the dresser's contents came into view.

"Wait a second!" Gloria said. "Over there, on the left hand side. It looks like a wad of cash."

Ruth shifted the camera and zoomed in. Sure enough, sitting next to the television set was a small stack of folded money.

"We suspected Libby Thornton gave Sean Brodwell Andrea's home address during their last meeting. What if she gave him money?" Gloria asked.

"What if Sean was the Thornton's drug supplier and he was blackmailing them to keep quiet?" Brian said.

"It makes sense. The drugs, the cash, the hand off," Ruth said.

"Perhaps the Thorntons, tired of being blackmailed, decided to hire a hit man to take Brodwell out," Margaret said. "So they hired Smooth Hand Luke."

They finished watching the rest of the footage, along with the footage of the restaurant where they caught a glimpse of the Thorntons inside Barnacle Bill's Seafood Restaurant. Libby Thornton appeared extremely nervous when the couple emerged.

"This whole fiasco is tied to the Thorntons, somehow," Gloria said. "I'm going to confront them in the morning, tell them I know they purchased illegal drugs from Sean Brodwell. I'm also going to tell them I think he was blackmailing them and they were paying him off in cash."

"Don't forget to mention hiring a hitman," Brian said.

"Smooth Hand Luke," Lucy, Rose, Ruth, Dot and Margaret said in unison.

Alice shook her head. "I still no believe Mr. and Mrs. Thornton are killers."

Gloria watched as Ruth disassembled her projector and packed up her other equipment, all the while plotting to confront the Thorntons first thing the next morning.

Chapter 22

Gloria stepped inside the Ocean View Resort lobby and gazed around. She had tossed and turned all night, wondering what Andrea would say when she found out Gloria confronted her parents with the accusation they were purchasing illegal drugs. She pushed the nagging thought aside and focused on her game plan.

Brian, who refused to let Gloria confront the couple alone, made his way over to the small sitting area off to the side to wait.

Gloria eased in behind a lush potted plant near the elevators. She stood there for what seemed like forever and her hip started to ache.

She shifted her feet and glanced at her watch. It was ten-thirty a.m. Brian and Gloria had already been there a couple of hours and she was starting to get odd stares from the hotel's bellhops as they passed by.

Gloria was about to give up and began making her way across the lobby to where Brian sat reading the morning paper when she spied the couple emerging from the bank of elevators.

She retraced her steps and stopped abruptly in front of them. "We need to talk."

Libby Thornton curled her lip. "What are you still doing here? I thought you would be on your way home, now that Andrea left."

"You know full well Brian Sellers is unable to leave the island until police have cleared him as a suspect in Sean Brodwell's murder."

Brian stepped into view and directly behind Gloria. "Hello Mr. and Mrs. Thornton."

Libby ignored Brian and focused her attention on Gloria. "We're late. We're on our way to meet friends for brunch at the country club."

"You were buying street drugs from Sean Brodwell before his death," Gloria whispered.

The panicked look on Libby Thornton's face told Gloria everything she needed to know. She had hit the nail on the head. She hurried on. "I think he was blackmailing you to keep quiet so you hired a hitman to take him out."

"That's absurd," David Thornton sputtered. "We had nothing to do with Sean's death."

"Is that why you were talking to Smooth Hand Luke over at Barnacle Bill's Seafood Restaurant last night?" Gloria asked. "Sean met with Luke before his death. Maybe you hired Luke to kill Sean and it was time to pay up."

Libby Thornton turned white as a ghost and she clutched her husband's arm. "Make them go away."

"We did not hire Luke to kill Sean Brodwell," David Thornton insisted as he wrapped an arm around his wife's waist. "What do you want from us?" he asked grimly.

"We want you to tell the police what you know. Even if you didn't have Brodwell murdered, he was blackmailing you. Maybe he was blackmailing Luke and Luke murdered him," Brian said.

"Why were you meeting with Luke at Barnacle Bill's last night?" Gloria asked.

"Because we knew Sean had met with him and wondered how much the man knew about us," Libby admitted. "Luke was Sean's..." Her voice trailed off.

"Supplier," David Thornton said. "Sean met with Luke for a business transaction."

Brian rubbed the stubble on his chin and rocked back on his heels. "So you paid Luke off to keep quiet."

"Sort of." David Thornton said. "Look. Let's move over to a quiet spot."

The four of them stepped outside and to the right of the hotel's entrance. "Libby is addicted to painkillers. She can only get so many to ease her back pain after being hit by a car while crossing Seventh Avenue in Midtown Manhattan a couple years ago. Sean and his parents are members of our local country club. One afternoon, we struck up a conversation with Sean and he offered to uh...help us out."

"We knew one of his connections was here on Nantucket so we invited him to join us. When we found out Andrea had decided to fly out to see us, we didn't dare mention Sean was here since Andrea didn't care for him." Libby gave Brian a quick glance. "It wasn't planned."

David Thornton clenched his fists. "We saw another side of Sean when he arrived. He knew Andrea did not know about her mother's...suffering. He began hinting around it would be a shame if Andrea found out. Finally, he outright told us he wanted ten thousand dollars cash to keep quiet."

"So you paid for his silence," Gloria said.

"Yes," Libby said. "We paid him to keep quiet. The last payment was made the day he died, but I assure you we had nothing to do with his death."

Somehow, Gloria believed Libby Thornton. Perhaps it was because she couldn't fathom someone as sweet and loving as Andrea having parents capable of murder.

"If you didn't kill Sean, who do you think did?" Brian asked. "Luke?"

"That would be our guess," David said.

Gloria remembered how Lucy had mentioned the mysterious death of Luke's girlfriend on his yacht. "I think there's one more clue we need to dig into. It appears Smooth Hand Luke is not only a drug supplier and extortionist, he could also be a killer."

She turned to Brian. "Let's head back to the motel."

Libby Thornton's hand trembled as she reached out and grasped Gloria's arm. Her eyes shined with unshed tears. “Please, don’t tell Andrea. I...”

A wave of sympathy washed over Gloria. “Mrs. Thornton, you and I may not see eye-to-eye but it is not my place to discuss this with your daughter.” She shifted her gaze to Brian.

“Mine either,” he said.

“Thank you both,” Libby said. She let go of Gloria’s arm and turned to face Brian. “I’ve treated you disrespectfully and for that I am sorry. I hope we can start over.”

“Of course,” Brian said graciously. “Mom.”

Gloria chuckled.

Libby gasped and then grinned.

Even David Thornton laughed.

Libby had one last thing to say. “I...would go to the police, Brian.” She gave her husband an uneasy glance. “It’s just that in our social position...”

Brian lifted his hand. "I understand. You don't want to air your dirty laundry." He shrugged. "It's okay. Maybe if you could drop by the station and put in a good word for me."

"Of course," David Thornton said. "The chief of police is a friend of mine. I'll see what I can do."

Brian and Gloria slowly exited the hotel property. "I'm missing something here. I know I am," Gloria said. "We need to research the accidental death of Luke's girlfriend. I don't ever recall hearing Luke's last name."

When they reached their motel room, Gloria found a note tucked in the door. She unfolded the note and handed it to Brian. "I left my glasses inside. What does it say?"

"It's from Ruth. She said they went over the video footage one more time this morning and Lucy thought she found a clue so they were headed back to Barnacle Bill's restaurant to have a look around."

"I wonder what kind of clue," Gloria said. She slipped her keycard in the door and then pushed it open. She dropped her purse on the couch and headed to her laptop to turn it on. "I'll let this warm up while I freshen up."

When she emerged from the bathroom, she settled in front of the computer and opened the search bar. "I don't know the girlfriend's name." She sent a text to Lucy to see if she recalled Luke mentioning the woman's name. Lucy quickly replied:

"Her name was Miranda and I remember thinking it reminded me of Miranda Rights. He said she drowned near Martha's Vineyard. Gotta go. We're onto something."

Gloria thanked her before typing drowning death, Miranda, and Martha's Vineyard in the search bar. She hit enter and scrolled the screen. On the second search page, she found a small news story. It was almost two years old. It talked about the mysterious death of Miranda

Farver of Hyannis, Massachusetts, who drowned while on Luke Chalton's yacht during a storm squall.

Although the authorities suspected foul play, no one was ever charged, including Mr. Chalton, for Ms. Farver's death, claiming insufficient evidence.

Gloria's pulse quickened as she read the last paragraph:

"Local Nantucket business owner, William Harding, owner of Barnacle Bill's Seafood Restaurant was the only other passenger on board the yacht, The Fathom, and he was quickly cleared of suspicion by the Nantucket Police Department.

Gloria blinked rapidly as she stared at the screen. It dawned on her what she'd been missing, the small clue she'd overlooked. "Luke Chalton aka Smooth Hand Luke didn't kill Sean Brodwell."

Gloria lunged for her phone. "We need to call Ruth. If they're over at Barnacle Bill's snooping around, they're all in danger."

Chapter 23

Ruth eased the van into a parallel parking spot a block away from the seafood restaurant. She turned to Lucy. "How can you be certain the guy we spotted walking past the crime scene and wearing a baseball cap was Bill Harding?"

"I already told you," Lucy patiently explained. "It was the small tattoo near the collar of his shirt. I could've sworn Bill Harding had a similar tattoo, right there." She pointed to the side of her neck. "He wanted to make sure Sean Brodwell was good and dead."

"Surely someone would've recognized him lurking around the time of Brodwell's death," Dot said.

"He was wearing a disguise to remain incognito," Lucy patiently explained. "He's a high profile local businessman. Someone would have recognized him."

"There's still the possibility it could have been Luke," Margaret said.

"That's why we're here." Lucy reached for the door handle. "We need hard evidence, something to link Harding to Brodwell's death. Who's up for a dumpster dive?"

Margaret wrinkled her nose.

Ruth shook her head. "Designated driver. I'm driving the getaway vehicle."

Rose shook her head. "I went on your last exploit. It's someone else's turn."

"I'll go," Dot said in a small voice.

"You already had a run in with the cops," Lucy said. "We can't chance a second confrontation. If we get caught, the police will arrest you."

All eyes turned to Alice. "Oh Miss Lucy. You know how much I care for Mr. Brian, but a dumpster?"

"I knew you'd step up to the plate." Lucy slid the side van door open and hopped out. "Whoops! Almost forgot my party pooper."

"Party pooper?" Ruth lifted a brow.

"My gun," Lucy said as she reached in her purse. She pulled out the small handgun and tucked it into the waistband of her jeans before she untucked her shirt to cover the weapon. "I wish I'd brought some gloves."

Ruth didn't answer as she leaned across the passenger seat, reached inside the glove box and pulled out a pair of latex gloves. She tossed them to Alice.

"Thanks Ruth," Lucy smiled. She turned to Alice. "Let's go Geronimo."

Alice made a cross sign. "I hope you know what you're doing." She reluctantly followed Lucy out of the van.

The women stepped behind the van and strolled down the sidewalk. As they got close to the restaurant, Lucy spotted a gravel path that ran along the side. "Let's take this." The women veered off the sidewalk and crept along the path. It led to the edge of the marina.

Lucy and Alice made a hard left and followed along an unpaved alley until Lucy spotted the back of Barnacle Bill's Seafood Restaurant. Directly behind the restaurant were several trashcans, neatly lined up in a row.

Beyond that was a large, green double dumpster. "You stand at the front and keep watch while I check out the trash." Lucy slipped on the rubber gloves Ruth had given her and bent down as she crept along the back wall of the restaurant.

When she reached the trashcans, Alice, who hovered near the front of the building, gave Lucy a thumbs up.

Lucy gently lifted the lid on the first plastic trashcan. It was full of soda cans. She sifted through the top layer before closing the lid and moving on to the next trashcan.

The second one was full of recyclable paper products. “At least he’s environmentally friendly,” Lucy whispered to herself.

The next can was full of glass bottles. The only thing left was the large dumpster. Lucy carefully lifted the lid and lowered it off the back. She stuck one foot on the ledge and pulled herself up, peering over the edge.

The dumpster reeked of rancid meat and rotting fish. *Cough.* Lucy started to gag. She covered her face with one arm and gripped the edge of the dumpster with the other, as she teetered precariously on the ledge.

Something inside the dumpster caused her eyes to burn so Lucy hopped off the ledge. She stepped to the side in an attempt to slip past the dumpster when she accidentally kicked a stray beer bottle with the side of her shoe, sending it rolling down a small incline.

She watched in horror as the glass bottle picked up speed and collided with the side of the brick building. It made a sharp *thunk*. The noise echoed in Lucy's head. It sounded like a cannon.

Lucy's eyes widened as the back door of the restaurant flew open and Bill Harding pushed the screen door open. "What's going on out here?"

Harding's eyes met Lucy's eyes. He looked down at the rubber gloves she was wearing and then at his open dumpster. "You were digging around in my trash?"

"I uh." A rush of adrenaline shot through Lucy. She did the first thing that came to mind...run.

"Let's go!" she yelled at Alice, who was still keeping watch near the end of the building.

Alice took one look at Bill Harding and raced down the sidewalk. Lucy was right behind her.

Lucy didn't slow her pace as she reached in her waistband and pulled out her gun. She didn't plan to shoot Bill Harding unless he shot first, but she also didn't want her weapon, which was pressing into her ribcage, to go off accidentally.

Lucy could hear Harding's heavy steps grow louder. He was gaining on her. She ran toward Ruth and the van as fast as she could.

Lucy had one more corner, one more turn before she reached the van.

Up ahead, Alice flew off the edge of the sidewalk. She lost her footing, lunged forward and fell to the ground.

The side van door flew open. Rose bolted out of the van and in one fell swoop, reached down, scooped Alice up and whisked her into the van. The door slammed behind them.

Ping. A small noise ricocheted off the light pole. Lucy instinctively lifted her hands to cover her head. *Harding was shooting at her!*

Ping. She heard it again.

The van was close now.

PING. There was a third ping, this one much louder.

Lucy's feet pounded the pavement and she willed herself to move faster, but it felt as if she was moving in slow motion. She could see Ruth's terrified gaze through the driver's side window. She could feel Bill Harding breathing down her neck.

The sound of police sirens filled the air and drew closer.

Lucy flung herself around the side of the van at the same time a police cruiser, lights flashing and sirens blaring, sped through the intersection, one street over.

There was one more deafening *PING* and Lucy was certain Bill Harding was finally going to hit his mark...her.

The side door opened. Margaret reached out and yanked Lucy inside. Dot flung the door shut and flipped the latch to lock it.

Lucy rolled onto her back and clutched her chest as she gasped for air. "I thought I was a goner."

She rolled over, her eyes frantically searching for Alice. "Are you okay?"

Alice nodded, her eyes filling with tears. "Rose...she saved my life."

"Aw, it wasn't nothin'." Rose's face beamed as she waved her hand in the air.

Lucy's cell phone chirped. It was Gloria. "Hello?" A breathless Lucy answered.

"Where are you? Are you near Barnacle Bill's? You need to get out of there!" Gloria shouted. "Bill Harding killed Sean Brodwell, he may have killed Luke's girlfriend and if he finds out you're on to him, he's going to kill you."

"Now you tell me," Lucy groaned. "How did you get the cops over here so fast?"

"Cops? I didn't call the cops," Gloria said.

Lucy lifted her eyes and stared at Ruth who was grinning from ear-to-ear. "Nevermind. I think I know who did."

Lucy pulled the phone away from her ear. "Did you call the cops?"

Ruth shrugged. "I thought you could use a little help. I told them that someone was breaking into Barnacle Bill's Seafood Restaurant."

"I wasn't breaking in. I was searching the trash," Lucy said. "We need to get out of here before police realize the call was a false alarm and Bill Harding comes after me again."

Ruth shifted the van into drive. "I might take him out with my bare hands. That jerk shot my van!" She narrowed her gaze and stared at Lucy. "Or did you shoot my van?"

"Of course not," Lucy argued. "Harding shot it."

"Did he ding it?" Ruth asked.

"Gee Ruth, I should've stopped to check it out before climbing in the van," Lucy said sarcastically.

"We need to get out of here," Dot interrupted.

"I guess I'll have to wait until we get to the motel to check for damages." Ruth glanced at her side mirror and then pulled onto the street. "You didn't happen to see what kind of gun he was using?"

Lucy rolled her eyes. "It was loaded. That's all I know."

When they reached the motel, Ruth eased into the back of the parking lot. "I hope Harding doesn't start looking for us." Everyone hopped out.

Ruth was the last to exit the van. She climbed out, shut the door and then slowly wandered down the side of the van.

The rest of the group headed toward their rooms but Lucy hung back. She would feel terrible if Ruth's van was damaged. "I'm sorry Ruth. Your van took a hit for me."

Ruth dropped her hand and faced her friend. "I would rather have the van take a million hits than for a single bullet to graze one of my best buds."

"It looks like she made it through unscathed." Ruth, never one for displays of affection, hugged Lucy. "Now don't ever let it happen again."

Chapter 24

Brian, Gloria, Ruth and Alice marched into the police station and over to the counter.

"We believe we may have new information in Sean Brodwell's murder investigation," Brian told the officer behind the counter.

"We have already made an arrest," the man said calmly. "An informant turned the suspect in."

"Was it William Harding?" Gloria asked.

"I'm sorry. I can't divulge that information. I do believe Detective Flint and Chief of Police Grobe plan to hold a press conference later today."

"So I'm free to leave the island," Brian said. "It's over."

The four of them headed back to the van and climbed in. Gloria was relieved police had finally made an arrest. She only hoped they had arrested the right person.

The group spent the afternoon exploring the island, ate an early dinner and headed back to the motel to wait for the evening news.

When the five o'clock news aired, Gloria was on pins and needles. There was a breaking news story, and Detective Flint and Chief of Police Grobe appeared on the screen. While the two men addressed the camera, they flashed a picture of a solemn-faced William Harding in the corner of the screen.

Police didn't identify the informant, but Gloria suspected it was Luke Chalton. They explained that local businessman William Harding had been charged with Sean Brodwell's murder and they were re-opening the investigation into Miranda Farver's death based on new evidence.

After the story ended, Gloria turned off the television set. “I knew it!”

“How did you know?” Brian asked.

“Sean Brodwell was blackmailing the Thorntons. He met with Luke Chalton and somehow found out Luke was the middleman and the real kingpin was William Harding. Think of it. Barnacle Bill’s is in the perfect location. All of those yachts and fishing boats, coming in and out of the marina. Harding was smuggling drugs into the U.S. Luke was his mode of transportation.

Gloria continued. “Maybe Luke had a few too many drinks and told Sean Brodwell that Harding was the kingpin. Brodwell got the bright idea to blackmail Harding so Harding killed him.”

“What if it was Luke and he’s framing Harding?” Margaret asked.

“Nope. It’s not possible.” Gloria shook her head. “Luke has a set ‘business’ schedule. He arrives on the island Wednesday evening. He leaves early the next morning for the next leg of his trip. Brodwell was murdered a couple days later. It couldn't have been Luke. He wasn't here. Our waitress the first night at the restaurant confirmed that when she said Luke came in every Wednesday, sat at the bar, paid cash and visited with Harding."

"And Luke said the same thing to me," Lucy said. "Sean Brodwell isn't a local. The only people or place we can link him to is Luke Chalton, the Thorntons..."

Brian finished Lucy's sentence. "And Barnacle Bill's."

"I'm ready to go home," Brian said.

"Me too," Alice smiled. "It's time for the lovebirds to reunite."

"Not only that, we have an engagement party to throw," Gloria said. "We need to get you two married before anything else happens."

"Maybe we should elope," Brian joked.

"You can't do that," Alice said. "We will follow you."

"Vegas, here we come," Margaret quipped.

***

Gloria eased Annabelle into Andrea's driveway and stopped behind her young friend's pickup truck.

Brian, who was sitting in the passenger seat, reached for the door handle and then froze.

"What are you waiting for?" Lucy asked. "Get in there. Your fiancée is waiting on you."

"I-I'm nervous," Brian admitted. "What if she changed her mind again and this is the end?"

Gloria reached over and squeezed his hand. "Brian. If Andrea planned to end your engagement, she would've done it already. She came home. She came home to you. She also knows you drove halfway across the country with a carload of crazy women to bring her home."

"Not to mention a van load," Lucy added.

Brian rubbed his brow. "This whole clunk on the head and not remembering her has been nothing but a nightmare."

"Oh…grasshopper," Gloria joked. "Love and marriage is a rocky road, but you can do it. This was a test and you both passed." She nudged him on the back. "Now get in there and kiss and make up."

Brian grinned. "Yeah, you're right. Who wouldn't love this mug?" He tilted his chin and batted his beautiful blue eyes before swinging the door open and stepping out of the car.

He turned to Alice, who was sitting in the back seat. "Don't you want to go too?"

"Oh no." Alice shook her head. "I won't be home until later this evening. Pierce is waiting at Dot's Restaurant for me. We have a lot of catching up to do. Don't wait up for us."

Brian started to close the car door.

"Wait!" Alice shouted.

"Huh?" Brian swung the door open again.

"Stay away from the big bottle of love potion in the spice rack. It's for the honeymoon."

Brian rolled his eyes. "I'll be sure to steer clear Alice." He blew Alice a kiss and then closed the car door before strolling across the drive and to the front porch.

The front porch door flew open and Andrea flung herself into Brian's arms. They disappeared inside the house and the door closed behind them.

"Now that's what I call a happy ending," Lucy sighed.

The end.

The Series Continues...Book 15 Coming Soon!

If you enjoyed reading "Nightmare in Nantucket", please take a moment to leave a review. It would be greatly appreciated! Thank you!

Get Free Books & More

Sign up for my Free Cozy Mysteries Newsletter to get free and discounted books, giveaways & soon-to-be-released books!

hopecallaghan.com/newsletter

Cherry Cream Cheese Surprise Recipe

Ingredients:

From Scratch Pie Crust: (8 or 9 inch pie crust)

1/3 cup plus 1 tablespoon shortening (Crisco) OR

1/3 cup lard

1 cup all-purpose flour

½ teaspoon salt

2 to 3 tablespoons cold water

Steps: Cut shortening into flour and salt until particles are the size of small peas. Sprinkle in water, 1 tablespoon at a time, tossing with a fork until all flour is moistened and pastry almost cleans side of bowl (1 to 2 tablespoons water can be added, if needed.)

Gather pastry into a ball. Flatten the ball on a lightly floured cloth-covered board. (A hard, floured surface will also work.)

Roll pastry 2 inches larger than inverted pie plate using floured rolling pin. (Note: I use a lightly floured spatula to loosen the piecrust from the surface.)

Fold pastry into quarters, unfold and ease into lightly greased pie plate, pressing firmly against bottom and sides of plate. Trim overhang excess and then press fork tines along rim of pie plate.

Cream Cheese Layer:

8 ounces whipped cream cheese
½ cup white sugar
½ tsp. vanilla extract

Mix ingredients and spread on the bottom and sides of the piecrust.
Mix 1 tablespoon brown sugar and ½ teaspoon cinnamon together and sprinkle over top of cream cheese mixture.

PREHEAT OVEN TO 375 DEGREES.

Cherry Pie Filling:

4 cups fresh or frozen cherries, thawed (if frozen, make sure to drain juice after thawing)
¾ cup sugar
3 tbsp cornstarch or

Mix ingredients and pour on top of cream cheese/brown sugar and cinnamon mixture.

Topping:

2/3 cup packed brown sugar
½ cup all-purpose flour
½ cup oats
¾ teaspoon ground cinnamon
¾ teaspoon ground nutmeg
½ cup margarine or butter, softened

Mix ingredients and sprinkle over top of cherry mixture.

Bake 30 minutes at 375 degrees.

*For a quicker, easier version, substitute with a refrigerated (ready-to-bake) pie crust and 2 cans of cherry pie filling.

*Serve warm with ice cream...or eat a piece for breakfast with a fresh cup of coffee ☺ .

Made in the USA
Monee, IL
17 May 2020

30958456R00171